'We can open out the sleeping bag and pull it over us.'

'Us?'

'Us,' she repeated firmly. 'If we're to be fit enough to travel tomorrow we've got to stay warm, and while sleeping with a total stranger isn't something I'd choose to do, tonight we've got no choice in the matter.'

She hoped she sounded more matter-of-fact than she felt and, although she was still busying herself with her padding routine, she couldn't help but sneak a peek at him.

'You're the nurse!' he said lightly, but she caught a gleam of what looked like laughter in his eyes, and would have paid good money to know what he was thinking.

And even better money to know who and what he was, this man who'd fallen slap bang into her life.

THE AUSTRALIAN DOCTORS

**Identical twins, identically single—they're about
to learn there's more to life than medicine!**

Identical twins Tom and Grant Hudson have had their
fair share of women problems but they're about to be
discovered by two women who will change their lives
and their outlook on love and marriage.

In *Found: One Husband* Sam Abbot literally stumbles
across Tom in the Australian rain forest. Injured, and
with amnesia, he doesn't know who he is, where he is
or how he got there. Fortunately for him Sam is a
nurse—she will save his life—and change it for ever.

In *Claimed: One Wife* neurosurgeon Grant Hudson
is against fraternisation amongst his medical team.
He has his reasons; they're hidden in his past.
But Dr Sally Cochrane is enough to make him break
all his own rules. A man can only resist so much!

**Next in this duo featuring
the fabulous Hudson brothers
CLAIMED: ONE WIFE
by Meredith Webber
May 2001**

FOUND: ONE HUSBAND

BY
MEREDITH WEBBER

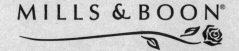

MILLS & BOON®

All the characters in this book have no existence outside the imagination of the author, and have no relation whatsoever to anyone bearing the same name or names. They are not even distantly inspired by any individual known or unknown to the author, and all the incidents are pure invention.

First published in Great Britain 2001
Harlequin Mills & Boon Limited,
Eton House, 18-24 Paradise Road, Richmond, Surrey TW9 1SR

© Meredith Webber 2001

ISBN 0 263 82656 2

Set in Times Roman 10½ on 11¾ pt.
03-0401-48427

Printed and bound in Spain
by Litografía Rosés, S.A., Barcelona

CHAPTER ONE

HE DIDN'T exactly drop from the sky. It was more a slithering, bumping descent, but the effect was much the same.

One minute Sam was rock-hopping quietly up the stream, revelling in the solitude, the splash and gurgle of the crystal-clear water as it scurried around the rocks, the occasional cries of birds in the thick rainforest which crowded the right-hand side of the creek.

Then suddenly there was this body, landing half in and half out of the water, right in front of her.

'Damn the man!' she muttered to herself, protesting the interruption to her blissful escape while shrugging off her backpack and hurrying forward to tend to him anyway.

There was an awful lot of him, she realised when she reached the small ledge that had prevented the top half of his torso landing in the creek. Too much for her to move on her own.

She peered upwards where snapped-off bushes and a scrape of loose stones marked the path he'd taken, and tried to visualise the map of this section of the park.

'Anyone up there? Hello?'

But even as she called, she knew the hope was futile. The man's companion, had he had one, would have been doing his own calling out. Yelling down the cliff, anxious for the reassurance of a reply from his friend.

Or her friend.

A stray sunbeam picked out the gold band on the man's left hand.

Her husband?

The thoughts jostled in Sam's head while her eyes did an initial survey of the inert victim. He'd landed on his side and she left him that way, reluctant to move him before she'd checked his injuries. It was close enough to the recovery position anyway.

He was definitely alive, as he was breathing, his chest rising and falling with a steady, reassuring rhythm beneath a faded khaki shirt which had seen better days. There was no blood spurting from open wounds—no open wounds that she could see if she discounted a multitude of abrasions. A hairy growth of curly brown beard had probably protected the lower half of his face, while the thick, overlong and slightly darker brown hair might have provided padding for his head.

She ran her fingers through her own short crop of rusty blonde curls and wondered if the curling of his beard bothered him as much as her wayward hair had always aggravated her. Not that hair was of the slightest importance at the moment! Was she thinking about it to put off the moment when she had to bring another sense into play in assessing his injuries? That of touch?

Come on! You touch patients every day of your working life. Touch the man! Feel his pulse.

She knelt on the ledge and wondered whether she'd feel a pulse beneath his chin. Find a chin beneath the beard? Went for the wrist instead, not moving his arm but feeling beneath the frayed, buttonless cuff of his shirt.

It was slow. Very slow, considering hers was racing and she would imagine most people, on falling down a cliff, would have reacted with some slight elevation in their heartbeat.

She lifted one eyelid and then the other. No obvious difference in pupil size but she had a torch in her backpack—she'd check reaction when she'd finished her physical examination.

Skull first. Setting aside her own lingering annoyance that her all-too-brief holiday had been disrupted, she thrust her fingers gingerly into the dark locks, pressing lightly against his scalp, feeling for contusions, for a movement in the bone that would suggest a fracture.

As far as she could tell, it was all intact, but if medical people had been able to diagnose cracked bones by feel, X-rays would never have been invented.

Sam moved on, running her hands down his body, lean and sinewy, and in one piece, if touch could judge. Then, listening for crepitus, that awful sound of bone scraping on bone, she gently moved his arms.

From his waist down he was in the water and the instinctive urge to somehow haul him out was countered by a fear he could have sustained spinal injury and any movement might exacerbate the damage.

She should go for help, but she was a day's walk from the nearest habitation and in the meantime the man might regain consciousness—or worse, part-consciousness—and wander off. Fall down another cliff. There were any number to choose from in the area, including the one she'd scrambled up a hundred yards farther along the creek.

Her immediate dilemma was solved by the man himself. He groaned and shifted, moving his legs, then moaning as if the movement caused him pain. But his legs had definitely moved. In fact, his pelvis had also moved for there was dampness spreading across the dry stones on the edge of the creek where he'd lifted his hips out of the stream.

'Hello! Can you hear me? Wake up. Talk to me.'

It wasn't standard recovery-room procedure for unconscious patients but Sam's anxiety level was rising as the deepening shadows over the creek reminded her that the sun was sinking. Night fell swiftly in the rainforest and moving anywhere in the darkness would be suicidal.

She looked around her, wondering where she could pitch her tent if they had to stay right here until morning. On this side, the cliff down which the unwelcome intruder had fallen rose steeply, while on the other, the growth was so thick, its tangled vines kissed the water.

'Talk to me!' she repeated, almost yelling the words in her despair.

'What about?'

She looked around, certain the man couldn't possibly have said the words. Whoever had been with him must have somehow scrambled down the cliff.

As far as she could see, they were still alone, so she turned her attention back to her patient.

'What did you say?' she demanded, watching lips she could barely discern in the hairy growth, hoping for movement.

'Jocelyn.'

The lips did move but only minimally, so the word sounded distorted.

'Jocelyn! Is that your name?'

Sam knew it more as a woman's name, but she had a vague feeling it could also be a man's. And who was she to argue with unisex names?

'Jocelyn?' she repeated, bending closer so she could see more of his face.

Which was when his eyes opened, and although she'd seen them earlier her attention had been on pupil size, not blueness. Bright blueness like the wedge of sky she could see above the creek.

'I'm Sam,' she said, as the eyes tried hard to focus on her face. 'What's your name?'

It was stupid conversation to be having, but Sam knew

she needed him conscious if she was to have any hope of getting him out of the wilderness area.

Or getting a rescue team in.

He was frowning at her, the blue eyes shadowed by lowered eyelids and a curtain of lashes a darker shade than his hair. Almost black, in fact.

'Is it Jocelyn?' she prompted, and the creases between his equally dark eyebrows deepened.

'Jocelyn's a sissy name!' he muttered crossly at her.

'Well, forgive me for breathing!' Sam shot back. 'I'm only trying to help!'

He looked at her then, really looked at her, and if anything the frown grew fiercer.

Arguing with him wasn't going to help, Sam reminded herself. Calm down—be professional.

'Perhaps Jocelyn's your wife,' she suggested, then watched as the frown developed into a black scowl.

'Pigs!' he said.

'And pigs to you, too!' Sam snapped, then she weakened. 'Look here, mate! I'm trying to help you. You've tumbled down a cliff in the middle of nowhere and I'm your only visible means of support. Somehow I've got to get the two of us out of here. Could you, please, at least try to get with it?'

His lips moved again, but this time it was to reveal strong white teeth. And the blue eyes were twinkling in a most beguiling manner. The man was smiling at her.

'No wife,' he said forcefully. 'Even though I was offered two pigs.'

He was either so satisfied with this response, or so worn out by the effort of talking, that his eyes closed and Sam felt him slipping away from her.

'Oh, no, you don't,' she told him, seizing his arm and dragging his wrist around so he could see his own left hand.

'You stay awake. And look at this. It's a wedding ring. You must have a wife.'

He opened his eyes and gave her a pained look, then mumbled again about pigs.

'That might be one reference too many to pigs in conjunction with wives!' Sam told him, as the eyelids drooped again. 'I've a good mind to leave you here on your own. You can take your chances with the cliffs!'

As if in response to her threat, the hand she'd waved in front of his face moved and she felt his fingers grasping hers, holding on tightly, like a child who didn't want to get lost in a crowd. It was cool, that hand, and slightly calloused, yet she felt, had their situations been reversed, she'd have found it comforting.

The thought made her feel more kindly towards him and she tried again for a verbal response. Nothing. Perhaps she should put her time to better use by getting the rest of him out of the water. Now his hips were resting on the edge, it should be easy to tackle the legs. If she moved the lower one, the right one, first, then eased the other up on top of it so he was lying curled on his side…

First detach his hand.

This proved difficult as the long, thin fingers tightened when she tried to disengage hers, and she had to pry them back, one by one.

'I'll hold it again soon,' she promised him, as this unspoken dependence on her touched her heart.

Before moving either limb, she ran her hands down each one, feeling through the thick wet material of his dirty, patched camouflage trousers for any obvious misalignment of bone.

No obvious breaks.

The plan worked well with his right leg, although with all the paddling around in the creek she was forced to do to get a good hold she was now as wet as he was. But when she lifted his left leg, gripping the damp trousers where she thought his calf would be, he stirred and groaned deeply as if the movement was causing him pain.

Sam lowered it gently and knelt in the shallow water, pushing the trouser leg up so she could see what was what.

His lower leg was intact, the femur forming a nice straight ridge, but his foot hung at a crazy angle, a clear indication all was not well with his ankle. Further examination showed it had already swollen inside his tough, scuffed hiking boot.

'If I leave your boot on for support and things swell more, it could constrict the blood supply to the rest of your foot,' she told her unconscious patient. 'And if I take the boot off and strap the ankle, you won't get it back on again, and without its support you'll have less chance of walking out of here!'

He was no help, although she sensed he might have heard her voice for he stirred and she thought she heard him murmur Jocelyn yet again.

'She must be your wife!' Sam told him, while her fingers probed the swollen tissue above the boot. 'Poor thing! Your wife, not you!'

Though why, apart from the pig's remark, she should be feeling empathy for his wife, she didn't know.

'Because you're a nuisance to me, I guess,' she admitted honestly. 'Which is most unfair of me!'

Deciding it was better to tackle his injury while he was still unconscious, she crossed to where she'd dropped her pack and dug around in it until she found her first-aid kit. Then, armed with sharp scissors and an elastic bandage, she returned to her patient.

Getting the boot off was the hardest part, and in the end

she had to resort to the kit again and use a scalpel and new blade on the tough leather before she could ease it off.

'Not a bad idea anyway,' she told her comatose patient. 'Maybe after a bit more surgery on the leather I'll be able to put it back on and give the joint some support.'

His ankle was very swollen, the bruise already coming out, turning patches of pale skin a purplish blue. She bound it carefully, then rested his left leg on top of the right so that he was now lying, curled like a sleeping child, on the narrow ledge.

Only he wasn't sleeping. He was unconscious.

A major concern!

She moved back to the head end of her unexpected company and noticed a redness in the curling beard she hadn't seen earlier. Not russet red, but blood red. Blood-soaked red, in fact.

An oath she rarely used echoed around the pristine wilderness and, first-aid kit still gripped in one hand, she knelt to investigate. Damping her handkerchief in the creek, she mopped up the worst of the blood, but couldn't pinpoint the injury.

'Here's hoping this face fuzz isn't something you've taken a lifetime to grow,' she muttered as she snipped at the damp hair, seeking the source of the bleeding.

The injury was on his jawline, a gash about an inch and a half long, deep enough to be showing the white of bone beneath it.

'Scars are manly things for men to have,' she told him, her mind racing as she considered and discarded options.

No razor to shave the area around the cut. She'd have to scrape away what she could with a scalpel and then suture the skin together.

Or try to hold it together with plastic strips?

If she left it open he'd have a wider scar—which the

beard would hide. Or would it? Perhaps the hair wouldn't grow where the scar was and there'd be an unsightly gap.

'I don't even like beards so why the hell am I worrying about your face fungus?' Sam muttered at him, searching through the compact pack for an antiseptic solution and the sutures and needles she knew she had stowed into it.

Shaving even such a small portion of his skin with a scalpel was difficult, but fortunately he lay still.

He stirred as she splashed antiseptic liberally around the area, but as she neatly stitched and tied off sutures he remained immobile.

'Not much point trying to put something over that,' she decided, speaking her thoughts aloud automatically.

'Over what?' the man mumbled, his head turning towards her as he asked the question.

Perhaps it was the beard, the mass of brown, that made his eyes look so blue.

'Over the gash on your chin,' she told him, smiling to hide the strange twinge the eyes were causing her. 'Are you properly awake this time? Can you tell me who you are? What you're doing here?'

He looked beyond her to the trees, the sky, then back to her, and frowned.

'Where's here?' he asked, then must have decided he was at a disadvantage for he sat up suddenly, almost knocking Sam back into the creek.

'Hey! Steady on! I'm wet enough, thanks to you,' she grouched at him, grabbing at his shoulder as he swayed precariously towards the creek.

The bits of skin she could see on his face, beneath beard, blood and scratches, were a greenish white and for a moment she thought he'd pass out again. She propped him against the rock face down which he'd tumbled and held him steady while he took in great gulps of air through his mouth.

Then his breathing steadied and the mesmeric eyes snagged her attention once again.

'Did you hit me?' he demanded, shaking off her supporting hand and feeling at what must have been a tender patch on his scalp.

'No, but I've been tempted!' Sam told him. 'You fell from up there.'

He turned to gaze upward, then groaned and gripped his knee as he moved his legs to get a better view.

'Is your knee sore, too?'

'No, it's my ankle.'

He peered at the offending joint then looked back at Sam.

'You've bandaged it!'

The accusatory tone riled Sam, though she knew head-injured patients were often argumentative.

'Ten out of ten for observation,' she sniped at him, anxiety prickling beneath her skin like a rash turned inside out. 'Now, let's try the questions again. Who are you? And what were you doing before you tumbled down the cliff to ruin my holiday?'

'Why do you want to know what I was doing?' he demanded, a frown pulling his eyebrows almost together. 'Why should that matter?'

He's concussed, Sam reminded herself. Be patient with him.

'If you were walking with someone and fell behind, or perhaps walked on ahead, then eventually that someone might just report you missing, which means people would come looking for you and we will both be found.'

'Are you lost?' he asked, the frown deepening slightly.

Mad as well as concussed?

'No! Of course I'm not lost!'

'Then why would you want to be found?'

Sam sighed.

'If this is how you normally behave, then it's very doubtful anyone would ever report you missing. In fact, they'd probably take themselves to the nearest church to give thanks on bended knee that they've finally got rid of you.'

Then, having vented herself of a little spleen, she added, 'We'll both be found because I'll be with you. I can hardly go off and leave an injured man lying here in the bush.'

'But don't tempt you?' he said, accompanying the words with a slightly rueful smile.

Sam was so surprised she chuckled.

'I'm sorry. I *have* been grumpy, but I hardly ever get away from people and I've been looking forward to having these two days alone. So to have you tumbling down into my little bit of solitude kind of threw me.'

He looked around and the frown returned.

'You're out here in the jungle all alone? Couldn't you have found your solitude somewhere safer than this? Isn't it stupid to be clambering around here on your own?'

The condemnation in his voice killed the moment of empathy his little joke had produced.

'Only if I fall down a cliff,' she told him, standing up and stepping over his legs to get to her pack. 'Now, do you think we could stop discussing my presence here and get back to yours? Does anyone know where you are? Are people likely to raise an alarm if you don't return home tonight?'

She considered how far she'd walked today and amended the question.

'Or tomorrow night?'

He stared at her, his eyes wide—as if startled—then he shook his head and the frown became positively ferocious.

He lifted both hands and ran them through his hair, wincing as fingers must have pressed against the tender part.

'I don't know!' he said crossly. 'Actually, I have no idea. I can't remember if I was with someone or alone, or whether someone knows where I am. In fact, I don't know that either. Where am I?'

He did the fingers in the hair thing again, and glared at Sam as if she might be responsible for stealing his memory.

'You're in the Border Ranges National Park, but in a fairly remote area of it. I don't know the marked trails very well, but as far as I know there's no regular walking track at the top of the cliff. Could you have rock-hopped down the creek?'

The man looked around again, peering into the rainforest as if he expected it to tell him something.

'What border?' he asked, his voice lower now. Husky. Almost as if he was afraid.

'Queensland and New South Wales. The mountains are known as the Border Ranges although they have their own names. This is—'

'Queensland and New South Wales in Australia?' he demanded.

'Of course,' Sam told him, although now she was feeling the coolness of fear. Was he more badly injured than she'd thought? 'Where did you think you were?'

But he was looking around again, and didn't answer, instead turning back suspiciously.

'You're sure of that?'

'Quite sure.' She opened one of the side pockets of her pack and pulled out her plastic-coated map. 'See. Here's the border, and the mountains. I left my car down there where that dotted mark ends, and followed the creek up. I think we're at about this point. This narrow swirl of lines indicate the cliff.'

He all but snatched the map from her hand and pored over it, running his finger over the names he found.

'Are these towns? I've never heard of them.'

The suspicion she'd heard earlier had deepened.

'They're more like villages,' she said. 'Little settlements down in the valley. Did you want a town?'

He must have heard the tartness in her voice for he glanced up.

'A name,' he said lamely. 'The name of a town I might recognise.'

Sam closed her eyes as the realisation that she was stuck in the bush with an injured amnesiac dawned.

'Do you know who you are?' she asked, more gently now she considered the awful confusion he must be feeling.

She saw the answer in his eyes, in the desperate gaze he fixed on her.

'You don't know me?'

Sam shook her head, then reached out to touch his shoulder.

'Don't try to remember right now. You've taken a bad tumble and knocked yourself unconscious on the way down. Give yourself time. It will all come back to you if you don't start worrying about it.'

'You're guaranteeing that?' he demanded, and as she turned and looked at him, and saw the same question reflected in his eyes, she knew she couldn't lie.

'No, I can't,' she said quietly, 'but right now there's nothing we can do about your memory, so let's think about what we can do, which is getting out of here.'

He was silent for a moment, then he nodded and again she saw the hint of a smile.

'So, how do we go about that, Girl Scout?'

Sam decided it was her turn to frown. She peered up at the cliff down which the stranger had fallen, and confirmed her earlier opinion. There was no way she'd get up it without pitons, and preferably someone at the top belaying rope to her.

'If you've told someone where you'd be, then they'll come looking for you eventually. Were you carrying a pack? Do you remember that much?'

The frustration in his eyes answered her, and she realised she should be saving him angst, not causing more by asking questions he couldn't possibly answer.

With a final twinge of regret for the loss of her peaceful idyll in the bush, and for the time she needed to think seriously about Henry, she turned her thoughts to practical matters.

'I think we should head back towards my car. I'll leave a note here in case someone does come looking. We've already lost the sun and will only have about an hour's light. Hopefully, by then we'll have found a slightly better place than this to camp for the night.'

The man greeted these sensible pronouncements with a look of undisguised horror.

'What's the matter now?' Sam demanded.

'What do you mean by ''camp for the night''? Isn't there a track? Couldn't we keep walking? How far away can your car be?'

'Too far for you to make it tonight,' Sam told him. 'That's assuming you can actually walk. Sit there while I hunt around for a stout stick. You can lean on me when we can walk abreast but there are a lot of places where you'll have to manage on your own. A stick will help.'

She knelt down beside her pack again, fumbling through the folds of rain slicker and clothing until she found a plastic container and the shape of a plastic mug.

Reaching out to the creek, she filled the mug with water and passed it to the man, handed him two paracetamol tablets from her first-aid kit, then opened the lid on her 'energy food'.

'Here.' She put the container down by his side. 'Dried fruit and nuts. Eat some of these, take the tablets and drink plenty of water before we get going.'

She turned her attention to writing a note and sealing it in a plastic bag which she held down with a rock at the base of the cliff, but when he didn't acknowledge the snack she looked up, to find him peering at the water in the cup, the expression on his face holding equal parts of horror and distaste.

'What's wrong now?' Sam asked him.

'You can't drink water straight from a stream,' he told her. 'I might have lost my memory, but I haven't lost my mind. Not drinking the water is a basic rule of survival in the bush. You need sterilising tablets, or should boil it for at least ten minutes to get rid of any deadly micro-organisms lurking in it.'

'In *this* water?' Sam teased, scooping up a handful and drinking noisily. 'This water?' She splashed it over his face and watched the droplets sparkle where they landed in his beard. 'This is pure, clean, fresh water, totally uncontaminated by any…'

Another aspect of what he'd said struck her forcibly enough to stop her mockery.

'You don't remember your name but you know about deadly micro-organisms in water?'

'My brother's a brain surgeon.'

The reply came out so pat that Sam chuckled, then laughed, and had to hold her sides as an uncontrollable mirth gripped her.

'Oh, I'm s-sorry,' she stuttered, wiping tears from her eyes and trying to control the final fits of giggles. 'But you have no idea how funny that sounded. ''My brother's a brain surgeon!'' It's like little kids using ''My Daddy's a policeman'' as the final unarguable, unanswerable threat.'

But her companion, now that her eyes were free of tears and she could see him clearly, seemed more puzzled than offended.

'Now, why would I know that if I don't know who *I* am?'

'I don't know enough about amnesia to explain,' Sam said, 'but I do know there's not much of a link between micro-organisms in drinking water and brain surgery, so I wouldn't take the brain surgeon as gospel. Unless by chance you can remember this brother's name?'

She was teasing him again, but gently, hoping a little light-hearted joking might ease some of the inner turmoil he must be feeling.

'Take my word for it, the water is clean so drink plenty of it—eat some fruit. I'll be right back.'

He didn't reply, but he did lift the cup slowly towards his lips and, as Sam smiled and nodded her encouragement, took a few tentative sips.

Confident she could leave him on his own for a few minutes, she stepped nimbly from rock to rock across the creek, trying not to think of the places along the banks where it was impossible to walk.

How the man would manage rock-hopping with his injured ankle...

CHAPTER TWO

FINDING a stout stick was easy, but getting the intruder to his feet might be more difficult. Sam was considering the logistics of this when she came out of the trees, to find him peering suspiciously down at his wet trousers.

'I'm wet!' he said in the fractious tone she was beginning to think might be his usual mode of speech.

Sam crossed carefully, using jumbled rocks as stepping stones, then answered as she reached the other side.

'You fell into the creek.'

'Oh!' he said, and the relief in that simple syllable made her chuckle.

'You've lost your memory, not become incontinent,' she assured him. 'Now, take this.' She handed him the stick. 'And let's see if we can get you upright.'

She squatted down beside him.

'If you put your arm around my shoulders, and use your right leg for leverage, we should be able to manage.'

'I can stand up by myself,' he protested, all but pushing her away. But when he tried a solo effort he lurched dangerously to one side and Sam had to move quickly, slamming her body against his to prevent him falling back towards the water.

'Now shall we try it my way?' she asked, ignoring his mutterings as she slid her shoulder into his armpit and then braced herself, using her legs to lever him up as her body took his weight.

'This is ridiculous,' he told her once he was upright but slumped against the cliff and panting hard. 'I must be very

21

unfit. Perhaps that's why I was hiking around in the bush. To improve my fitness.'

But the words trailed away as he finished the sentence and the frown returned, directed at Sam.

'Who's Jocelyn?' he demanded.

Had he remembered something?

'Why do you ask?' Sam prompted.

'Because the name is hammering in my head. Who is she?'

Sam shrugged.

'You tell me and we'll both know. I'm assuming it's your wife—and don't say "pigs" again.'

His expression grew puzzled.

'Pigs?'

Sam smiled at his confusion.

'They featured in the earlier conversations we had,' she told him. 'It was like a reflex action. Those psychological tests people do, where you're asked to say the first word that comes into your head in response to the word the questioner gives you. I said "wife" and you said "pigs".'

She was teasing him, but it didn't work. Instead, his eyes grew wary, and the frown returned.

'I was offered two pigs,' he said slowly. 'But I'm sure I said no.'

Bizarre didn't begin to cover this situation, Sam decided, but if this pigs thing was something he remembered maybe she should pursue it in case it led to more revelations.

'Two pigs in exchange for your wife?'

'I haven't got a wife!' the man stormed, and Sam guessed that if he'd had a spare, uninjured foot he'd have stamped it. 'I've already told you that.'

'If you don't know who you are, then you can't possibly know if you've got a wife or not,' Sam told him.

'I know my brother's a brain surgeon so, of course, I'd know if I had a wife,' he argued.

'Ah, yes!' Sam scoffed. 'I'd forgotten the brain surgeon.'

She spoke lightly but she'd been studying him as she talked and she felt he'd regained enough colour in what she could see of his cheeks for them to try moving.

'In the meantime,' she said, 'perhaps we should think of a name for you so I can call you something.'

'Instead of "hey, you",' he said, and she had to smile at the little joke.

'Exactly,' she said, then she hitched herself to his side again. 'Do you want to see if you can take any weight on your left foot?'

He put it on the ground, and tentatively tilted his body, but the colour draining from his face told her this wasn't going to work.

'OK, hey you,' she said as lightly as she could, considering the worrying situation, 'you'll have to hop. Use the stick as one crutch and my shoulder as the other, and swing your injured leg along between us. When we get to places where we can't move side by side, I'll give you extra pain relief and we'll do the best we can.'

She propped him against the cliff again.

'Stay right there until I get my backpack on, then we'll be off.'

'You can't take my weight and that backpack,' he complained.

'Just watch me,' Sam told him. 'And stop arguing. Save your breath for staying upright.'

She tied the remnants of his boot to the outside of the pack, then settled the weight comfortably across her shoulders, before taking up a position close to his side.

'I'm not suffering from any communicable diseases,' she

told him, when he put his arm tentatively around her neck. 'Hang on tight, or we'll both go toppling over.'

They set out, struggling along the narrow ledge beside the creek, Sam in it as often as she was out of it, aware that her patient was putting more weight on his foot than was good for it.

'John Doe's the accepted name for unidentified bodies. Do you fancy John?' she asked him, hoping conversation would distract him from his pain.

'I'm not dead. At least not yet!' he muttered at her.

'Don't like John? What about Jack? Although Jack Doe doesn't have quite the same ring to it.'

'No wonder you're out here on your own,' he grumbled at her. 'No one in their right mind would put up with you for any length of time.'

'I should drop you right here,' Sam grumbled right back. 'And as I have no intention of calling you "hey, you" for however long we're joined at the hip like this, perhaps *you* can think of a name.'

Silence greeted this remark but after a few painfully slow steps farther down the creek he finally said, 'Well, I don't mind Sam.'

Sam chuckled.

'You can't have that one. It's already taken. And we can't both be called Sam. I did introduce myself earlier so the name must have lingered in your subconscious. I'm Sam Abbot.'

'How do you do?' 'hey, you' said, with an automatic politeness which, for some reason, pleased Sam. 'And I'm…'

But again he stuck, cursing softly under his breath.

'Bill? Fred? Albert's nice,' Sam suggested.

A huffing sound greeted her suggestions.

'Harry? Sebastian? Charlie?'

Sam found thinking of names for him made the going easier but her companion must have disagreed.

'Stop with the names,' he growled. 'Sebastian! Do I look like a Sebastian to you?'

'I've never met a Sebastian,' Sam told him, 'so I wouldn't know what they look like. Perhaps slightly shorter and fatter than you.'

It was a silly conversation but infinitely better than thinking of the weight around her shoulders and the ordeal that lay ahead.

'Jack! Did we already talk about Jack? Is that why it sounds right?'

'It enjoyed a fleeting mention,' Sam told him, peering ahead in the hope they'd find a place to rest before too long. 'But it's a good, solid, no-nonsense name. Are you happy to go with it?'

'Jack?' he repeated tentatively. Then he nodded. 'Yes, Jack will do nicely.'

'Well, I'm glad we've got that sorted out,' Sam said, then she pointed with her free hand. 'Now, see that rock? How about you settle on it for a few minutes while I do some reconnaissance?'

'I'm too heavy for you,' the newly named Jack decreed. 'This is a stupid idea. You should leave me here and go ahead on your own. Get help.'

'Don't tempt me,' Sam teased, then regretted the light-hearted words as the body so close to hers tensed and she felt him trying to distance himself from her. 'Actually, I might go on ahead tomorrow but until then you're stuck with me.'

'Why not until tomorrow?'

Jack eased himself onto the rock she'd chosen and sighed with relief as he rested his injured foot on another small one nearby.

Sam shrugged off the pack again, and perched on top of it.

'You've bumped your head badly enough to cause concussion. You could suffer a delayed reaction of some kind and—'

'How do you know? Are you a doctor?'

'I'm a nurse,' Sam explained, not adding that her expertise was in theatre nursing and, more recently, some training in ICU. He'd probably be more reassured if he thought she had casualty or general nursing duties.

'Jocelyn's a nurse.'

The statement seemed to startle him as much as it surprised his audience of one.

'Maybe she's your sister,' Sam suggested. 'Medical family—brother a brain surgeon, sister a nurse.'

He peered suspiciously into her face.

'You're teasing me.' The accusation lost impetus, however, when he added, 'And your eyes are green. I don't think I've ever seen anyone with green eyes before. Not true green like that.'

'You can't remember your own name,' Sam reminded him, 'so how do you know what colour eyes you've seen?'

'I'd know,' Jack said firmly, then he smiled, and even with what she could see of that slight movement of his lips Sam felt a flutter of attraction in her veins.

Just as well the beard concealed a lot of his facial expression. She had a feeling the full effect of that smile might be devastating.

'I'll be back shortly,' she told him, heaving herself off the pack and heading resolutely away from the man. Others might talk about instant attraction, but she knew it didn't exist. Not for her. She was the slow-and-steady type. Sensible.

'Practical,' she reminded herself, hoping if she heard the

word aloud it might be more effective. 'And right now you've got to sort out a way to get him down the cliff.'

She'd managed to scramble up it on the far side of the waterfall, but she doubted whether Jack would make it down that route. Perhaps there was another, slower way, through the rainforest.

She searched for half an hour, but every likely track was cut off by a sheer drop or impenetrable undergrowth. Eventually she admitted defeat and made her way back to the creek and surveyed the waterfall. On this side, the ground was less steep. If—

'I can get along perfectly well like this,' a deep voice announced, and she turned to see her 'patient' sitting not ten yards from where she stood. He had the stick she'd found for him hooked through a strap on her pack and had obviously hitched himself along the ledge on his bottom, going backwards to protect his injured ankle and dragging her pack with him as he inched his way along.

Instinct made her want to scold him, until she realised he'd solved her dilemma of getting him down to the lower level.

'You can't go backwards down here,' she told him, 'but that mode of travel is probably the only way to do it.'

She moved towards him as she spoke, not wanting to yell above the sound of the falling water.

'Are you sure you're OK? Not hurting your foot too much?'

He shrugged a reply and she realised it was all she'd get from him. Bumping along was obviously causing him a deal of pain but talking about it wasn't going to make it better.

Sam hefted her pack to her shoulders again and took his stick.

'You'll be better off with both hands free,' she told him.

'I'll go first, then you'll have to slither down behind me. If you wait at the top until I drop off my pack at the bottom, I can come back up and help you.'

'I won't need help,' he told her firmly. 'And it's stupid for you to go first. What if I come crashing down and take you with me? Then we'll both be injured.'

'You won't come crashing down,' Sam told him, 'because I'll be helping you. Now, while I go down, you can wriggle your way to the top and turn around so you can at least see where you're going.'

'Are you always this bossy? Is it a nurse thing?'

Sam felt her spine stiffen at the word 'bossy' but decided to ignore it. She took the attack to him instead.

'Why, is Jocelyn bossy?'

As soon as the brows drew together in the now familiar frown she knew she'd beaten him.

'I don't know,' he said, but instead of sounding cross it came out as a gruffness and made her ache for him as she understood the depths of his confusion.

'Don't let it worry you,' she said, and touched him gently on the shoulder. 'Let's concentrate on getting out of here.'

He glanced up, and she felt his eyes scanning her face, as if trying to read something in it.

'Sam of the green eyes,' he said softly, then he nodded and she knew it was time to move.

With more haste than care, she slid and slithered down the steep slope. Instinct told her the newly named Jack wouldn't wait for her assistance. He had a way to go before he reached the top of the incline, but once there she was sure he'd press on. Probably come tumbling down and do further damage to his body.

And his head.

She dumped her pack and then, determined to help his

descent, she scrambled back up to the top, mentally noting hand- and footholds as she went.

His feet greeted her at the top, then he lifted his body forward until his legs dangled down over the drop.

'Get out of the way! We'll both be killed if I happen to slip.'

'I'm in charge here so stop giving orders,' Sam retorted. 'I've worked it out. The important thing for you to do is keep your weight well back. I'll guide your good foot to a solid rock or ledge, then you can squiggle down to it, finding your own handholds on the little shrubs or in crevices between the rocks, then I'll find the next foothold and the next and down we'll go.'

'Why do you need to guide my foot? I've lost my memory, not my sight. I can see places to put it.'

Sam sighed.

'The first dozen times you argued I put it down to the concussion, but now I'm beginning to think you're just plain argumentative. Which means the chances of anyone reporting you missing are becoming slimmer by the moment. Who'd want you back?'

He looked down into her eyes, but this time didn't argue. Instead, he did his slight smile thing and said, with mock humility, 'I'm sorry, ma'am. Please, explain.'

She ignored the smile. This was time for practicalities, not smiles. And instant attraction didn't exist!

'Remember what I said about keeping your weight back. In order to look down and find a foothold, you'd have to tip forward. It shifts your centre of gravity and makes a tumble far more likely.'

'I'm going down facing outwards, not facing towards the cliff?'

He sounded so incredulous that Sam dithered.

'I thought that would be the least painful way for your

ankle,' she said, frowning as her eyes scanned his body, trying to imagine it making the tricky descent. 'Facing in, you could jar it and a sudden jab of pain could distract you.'

'And send me plummeting to the bottom?' Once again his eyes studied her for a moment, but in the end he nodded. 'Perhaps you're right.'

He let her take his foot and guide it to a point above the roots of a stronger than average plant.

'Now slide carefully down to there until you're squatting on your heel.'

'Easier said than done,' he muttered at her, as small stones slid loose and accelerated his downward slide.

'It's OK, I'm on solid ground, I can slow you down.'

It worked, much to Sam's satisfaction, for things often seemed sensible in theory but in practice went horribly wrong.

The horribly wrong part came a little later when they still had more than half the steep slope to conquer and she failed to find a solid resting place for his foot.

'I'm stable, so you'll have to use my knee,' she told him, and turned so her bent knee would provide support for him.

'I won't use your knee,' Jack argued, squatting on his right heel two feet above her, his left leg dangling uselessly in front of him. 'I'll break it! Or send us both to the bottom. There has to be another way.'

'Letting you fall is all that comes to mind,' Sam told him tartly. Her legs, back and shoulders were all protesting at the effort of keeping her own balance while guiding him down the slope. 'Or I can leave you there until the rock gives way. Or we can both stay here and argue until it's dark then drop off when exhaustion overtakes us halfway through the night. Or—'

'Oh, hush up!' he muttered at her. 'I know we can't stay

here. I'll use your damn knee if that will make you happy. Just stop your nagging.'

'I do not nag!' Sam said huffily. 'Never! I was merely pointing out the alternatives.'

She wriggled her feet to make sure they were on solid ground, then bent her knee and reached up to take his foot.

'Are you holding onto something?' she asked.

'Yes. The trunk of a young palm tree. I'm imagining it's your neck so I'll grasp it tightly!'

She shot him a wrathful glare and guided his foot down to rest on her knee, then tensed, expecting his weight to follow.

It didn't.

'Guide my hand to another handhold,' he barked, waving his left hand in her face. 'I'll try to keep most of my weight on my arms until my foot can reach whatever you're standing on.'

Sam took his hand and placed it around the knotted roots of a tiny shrub.

'Ouch! That's got prickles.'

'Prickle wounds we can fix,' she reminded him. 'Come on.'

'Now I need something lower for my right hand,' he told her, staring grimly up towards the sky as he obeyed her insistence to keep his weight back as far as possible.

'Slide down first,' she told him.

'No way! You find somewhere for my hand and I'll hang until I can reach a foothold.'

'And what if your arms give way?' Sam muttered, but she found a handhold for his right hand and swung across his body to help him grasp it as he released the palm trunk and cascaded down towards her. Her knee straightened in the process and she was now spreadeagled across him. Detaching herself wasn't going to be easy.

'Can you feel a ledge under your right foot?' she asked him, addressing the top button of his shirt.

'What's this?' he asked, pressing down hard on her instep.

'My foot,' she told him grimly. 'I'll wriggle it to the left and you'll only have about an inch to drop to feel the ledge under your foot. Let go of the prickle bush, it's higher. Your right arm should anchor you.'

It must have been more than an inch he needed to drop, for he came to rest with his curly beard directly in front of her, and his bright eyes looking quizzically down into hers.

'Cosy?'

'I'm making sure you don't fall off,' she told him, but there was something else she couldn't quite explain going on as well. 'If your foothold is secure, I'll let go now.'

Which was when it all fell apart. As she released the hold they'd shared on the small shrub, the foot she'd assumed was anchored safely on a ledge slipped, and she would have been the one to go hurtling downwards if his strong left arm hadn't clasped her to his body, holding her close while her feet scrabbled for somewhere to rest.

'OK?' he asked, when her diminishing struggles must have told him she was safe again.

'Yes, thanks,' she said, and felt heat creep into her cheeks as she looked up to let him see she meant it.

'Hold onto my belt as you lower yourself down,' he suggested, apparently as cool as she was flustered. 'You can't see where you're heading, clamped up against me like this.'

It made sense but it took a mammoth effort of will to tuck her fingers inside the belt of this total stranger.

Somehow they made it down, but conversation between them had ceased as the effort sapped their energy and the darkening shadows warned them not to dally.

A flat ledge of ground at the base of the cliff would provide a perfect place to camp for the night.

'It's not dark. We could keep going,' Jack objected—predictably—when Sam suggested it.

'No way!' she countered. 'This is it for us tonight. I'll look for some firewood, then you can take your turn at the Scout thing and get a fire going while I sort out food and sleeping arrangements.'

The logistics of sharing a one-man tent, a narrow foam mat and a single sleeping bag had been weighing on her mind for some time. As she trekked off into the forest in search of wood, they seemed overwhelmingly important. The nights, up here in the mountains, were cold, and maintaining body heat would be a priority.

Back on the ledge, she found that her companion had already started a small fire, setting it carefully within a circle of stones and using leaves and twigs he'd gathered from within arm's length of where he sat.

'Great! Most of the wood I've found is damp, but if we put one piece at a time on your little fire we can dry it out bit by bit.'

She stacked the wood beside his circle of stones, then smiled at him.

'Did you find anything else in your pockets when you were searching for matches? A wallet, for instance? Driving licence?'

He shook his head.

'I can't believe we didn't think to look earlier, when I was trying to work out who I was. Not that there was anything helpful. There was a compass in my shirt pocket, and some keys, but what they open is anybody's guess.'

He tossed them to her and she sorted through them, frowning as she went through once again, seeking what she felt was missing.

'There's no car key, yet you can't have reached this area without transport,' she muttered, not actually talking to him but speaking her thoughts aloud. 'There must have been someone with you. Someone who drove you here.'

A chill slid up Sam's spine and she shivered. She'd been joking about someone pushing him over the cliff.

'No apples, fruit bars, chocolate?' she asked. If he was on a day walk then his pockets were the obvious place to carry such supplies.

He shook his head. 'A box of matches, compass and those keys. Hardly being prepared, would you say?'

She grinned at the new Scout allusion. His mind couldn't be too badly affected by his fall if it could make connections like that.

'You might have had a pack. It's possibly at the top of the cliff.'

Or had his companion taken it? Got rid of evidence?

'Is that such a worry?' Jack's voice arrested her mind's flight into the absurd.

'Worry?'

'You were frowning most ferociously,' he explained. 'Not a good look on a face that's obviously meant for smiles and laughter.'

'S-smiles and laughter indeed,' she stuttered, although what she really wanted to say was, Don't talk to me like that. But she couldn't say it without acknowledging that his unexpected compliments added to her uneasiness. 'Isn't your fire going out?'

The diversion worked and while he blew on it, and cajoled his smouldering leaves back to life, she opened her backpack and began to empty it, spreading the contents around her on the flat ground so she could study what she had and how to make best use of the limited supply.

'If I spread one layer of the tent on the ground, then the

mat and a padding of clothes and fold the top layer of tent over that, it will give us the illusion of softness and we can open out the sleeping bag and pull it over us.'

She worked as she talked through her plan, glancing up as Jack echoed the final word.

'Us?'

'Us,' she repeated firmly. 'If we're to be fit enough to travel tomorrow we've got to stay warm, and while sleeping with a total stranger isn't something I'd choose to do, tonight we've got no choice in the matter.'

She hoped she sounded more matter-of-fact than she felt and, although she was still busying herself with her padding routine, she couldn't help but sneak a peek at him.

'You're the nurse!' he said lightly, but she caught a gleam of what looked like laughter in his eyes, and would have paid good money to know what he was thinking.

And even better money to know who and what he was, this man who'd fallen slap bang into her life.

CHAPTER THREE

As JACK coaxed the embers back to flickering flames, Sam spread her sleeping bag on the makeshift bed, then turned her attention to her meagre stock of food. Apart from fruit, her subsistence rations consisted of chicken-flavoured instant noodles, a packet of dried mixed vegetables—peas, carrots and corn—and some cracker biscuits. Hardly gourmet fare but it would save them going hungry.

'You really are a Girl Scout,' Jack said, watching her hitch a handle to the larger of the two metal dishes she could use as both saucepan and soup bowl. 'And a little stove as well.'

'I don't like lighting fires if I can help it,' she told him, not adding that if someone were looking for him, the smoke from tonight's fire might relieve anxiety.

'What do you think about, out here on your own in the bush?'

She glanced up from her preparations, surprised by the conversational switch. He was watching her as if the question went beyond the mundane—as if he really wanted to know.

Sam thought about it for a moment and discarded total honesty—after all, telling him about Henry would mean lengthy explanations. And might cause her to question why she'd put off marrying Henry for so long.

'Not much!' she finally declared. It sounded lame on its own so she expanded the statement. 'Well, actually, quite a lot, but it's more as if my mind drifts from subject to subject. Nothing too deep or meaningful. Most of the time

I'm looking around, breathing in the unpolluted air, listening to the bird calls, the splash and gurgle of the water—just revelling in the peace and beauty of it all.'

'Peace and beauty. It certainly has that,' he agreed, but the look he gave her suggested he didn't quite accept her explanation.

Or perhaps understand her motivation.

'Do you eat noodles and vegetables?' she asked, changing the subject herself to discourage further probing.

'I eat anything,' he said, so firmly he must have surprised himself as well as her for he added, 'Now, how can I know something like that if I don't know who I am?'

'Maybe a neurologist could tell you, but as we haven't one handy—' Sam carefully refrained from mentioning brain surgeons '—the best I can do is assure you that remembering some things is a good sign. My knowledge of amnesia is limited to two types—retrograde, which, if I remember correctly, is where you can't recall the events leading up to when you hit your head—'

'That's what I've got,' Jack said. 'I haven't a clue where I am or what I'm doing here.'

'Nor do you know who you are,' Sam reminded him. 'I think that's more likely to be the other one I know, which is post-traumatic amnesia, and it covers all the time from when you had the head trauma to when you finally remember everything.'

'Which may be never,' her companion said gloomily.

'Nonsense!' she told him, using her 'brisk nurse' voice. 'It will all come back to you.'

She busied herself preparing their meal, which was a better option than considering why the possibility of him not remembering should make her feel so upset. She'd use the little stove, which was easier than trying to balance the pot above the fire. It also meant Jack could keep feeding the flames rather than having to suppress them in order to cook.

In the end it was his silence that made her turn back towards him. The fire was burning well, but he wasn't feeding it. He was far too intent on unwrapping the carefully wound bandage from around his ankle.

'What are you doing?' she demanded. 'You shouldn't be disturbing it.'

'I'm having a look,' he said, his tone implying that it was his right to do exactly that.

'And I suppose you'll expect me to wrap it up again when you've finished looking,' Sam muttered at him.

'No, I think I can manage,' the infuriating interloper replied.

'Of course you can!' Sam iced the words with sarcasm. 'Your brother's a brain surgeon!'

Then she weakened.

'Actually, it's not a bad idea. You can put your foot in the water for a while, which should help reduce the swelling, then, when I bind it again, I'll try splints on either side of it, which might help keep it stable—'

'And allow more weight-bearing.' He finished the sentence for her, but not with the words she'd intended using.

'Forget weight-bearing until it's been properly set, and possibly for a few days afterwards,' she told him. 'From what I could feel, you've gone over on it, possibly before you fell. It seems like an abduction injury to me, where your leg has twisted inwards not outwards. That's likely to result in a fracture of the tip of the tibia and possibly the end of the fibula as well. There are ligaments that hold the end of these bones to the bones in your foot. These can snap or become displaced as well.'

Night was falling rapidly so she couldn't see his eyes, but she felt an intensity in the gaze he turned on her.

'Tibiofibular ligaments, right?'

The words startled her, until she realised that anyone who'd done a basic first-aid course would have known the name.

'Pretty easy to guess when I'd already named the two bones,' she told him, but he'd turned away and was stirring the fire, the rising flames revealing that his frown was back in place.

She touched him lightly on the shoulder.

'You're remembering more and more,' she said, her voice gentled by the compassion she felt for him. 'It will all come back in time.'

'Will it?' Jack demanded savagely, and she knew that if he'd been able to use his foot he'd have stood up and walked away from her, his tension demanding the release of movement.

But he couldn't move away, so she would. Leaving their meal simmering on the little stove, she found her torch then headed into the dark shadows of the rainforest. Ideally, she needed two ten-inch-long, flat pieces of a very light wood but, being reasonably certain she'd not find the ideal splints, a couple of straight sticks would do.

When she returned with a selection of four, he'd moved to the edge of the creek and had both feet in the water. As she approached, she saw him dip his handkerchief into the stream, then rub it over his face, beard and all, and down his neck.

'Bathtime?'

He turned and she caught a gleam of white that told her his mood had mellowed and he was smiling at her.

'Always wash before a meal. My mother must have taught me that.'

Sam returned his smile then, because smiling at him didn't seem like such a good idea, she checked on their meal. The noodles were done and the previously shrivelled and unappetizing-looking vegetables were now plump and colourful.

'Do you want to keep your foot in the creek while you eat or would you be more comfortable with it out? The food will keep if you want me to bind your ankle first.'

'Are you going to join me in the creek? If not, I think it would be extremely antisocial of me to eat with my back to you. Especially after I've spoilt your holiday.'

Sam thought he was probably teasing, but couldn't be sure. After all, she'd grumbled practically non-stop about him destroying her solitary adventure.

'I'll bind you up, then,' she said lightly, and found the small but super-absorbent towel she carried. 'With splints this time.'

He swung both legs out of the creek and presented his bare feet to her. He'd rolled his trousers up to just below the knee, and although his legs were tanned the warm nut brown of a man who spent a lot of time out of doors— while dressed in shorts—his ankles and feet were so white she knew boots must also be part of his everyday wear.

She'd already seen the left foot and had not been particularly affected by it, but the two together seemed incongruously pale and somehow vulnerable.

Forget vulnerability! Sam told herself, but her fingers trembled as she patted his foot dry.

He's lean and brown and probably as tough as teak, she told herself as she wrapped gauze bandages around the sticks she'd found, while mentally dissecting her reactions to him.

'A figure of eight around the ankle first, then around the sticks. I'll hold them.'

The words startled her into looking up. He was holding

the elasticised bandage he'd removed earlier, neatly rolled to make rebinding easier.

'So you know some first aid,' she teased. 'But don't let it go to your head. I'm the boss here, remember!'

He laughed, and the sound was almost as appealing as the splashing of the water in the creek.

Though she should be thinking about his injury, not his laughter.

Instant attraction was a myth.

She did the required figure of eight, keeping the bandage firm but not over-tight, but when he put the padded sticks in place and his fingers brushed against hers, her reaction was so strong she looked up again, wondering if he was doing it deliberately. Somehow transmitting a charge like an electric current from his body into hers.

'Only electric eels can do that,' she muttered to herself as she turned her attention back to stabilising his ankle.

'Pardon?'

'Talking to myself. There! You're done. I still wouldn't put weight on it but it might feel better. When you've had something to eat I'll give you a couple more painkillers.'

She stepped across his legs and knelt beside the little stove, found her second bowl and ladled a good portion of the food into it, then offered it to him.

'You can have the fork or the spoon,' she told him while he sniffed appreciatively at the makeshift meal.

'What? No silver service?' he said, choosing the fork, and again transmitting whatever it was in his body—only this time Sam had made sure their fingers didn't touch.

Yet the tingle rippled up her arm again. Perhaps he could make it arc from him to her, using the metal of the cutlery as a conductor.

Deliberately?

Surely not.

It had to be her own tension causing the disturbance. After all, she had more than enough to be tense about, what with the interruption to her short holiday and getting them both out of the rainforest safely.

They ate in silence, broken only when Jack said, 'I should have opted for the spoon. There's a lot left in the bowl but I can't get it with the fork.'

'Drink it straight from the bowl,' Sam told him. 'That's what they do in Asia where noodles are a big part of the local diet.'

She watched him raise the bowl, then the movement was arrested before the liquid reached his lips.

'Asia? You're sure we're not in Asia?'

'Quite sure,' Sam told him. 'The Border Ranges, between Queensland and New South Wales. I can guarantee that's where we are.'

She spoke confidently, but his confusion over where they were bothered her. It suggested he'd suffered a more serious head injury than she'd imagined. And if that was the case, there could be bleeding going on inside his skull right now, building up, pressing on the brain. He could go into a coma any minute and how was she supposed to relieve the pressure? Knock a hole in his skull? Use a stone to hammer a knife through the bone?

'Hello?' He rapped his knuckles gently against her forehead. 'Are you still with me or have you fallen asleep sitting up?'

Sam snapped off the terrifying images her own brain was screening for her, straightened to avoid any further physical contact between them, and tried to recapture the echo of whatever words he'd set free into the air. Wasn't auditory memory supposed to be better than visual memory?

Further conversation about Asia? Or a particular Asian country?

'I'm sorry. I was thinking of something else. What were you saying?'

She looked at him and saw the gleam of teeth that indicated he was smiling.

'Just that for some reason I keep thinking I'm in Asia. Not all of it, but South-East Asia. Sumatra comes to mind.'

'Perhaps Jocelyn lives there!' Sam offered.

'This is not a joking matter!' The smile disappeared and he snapped the words at her. 'Well, not for me!' he added in a milder tone, reaching out to touch her lightly on the arm by way of apology.

Sam edged farther away. She'd tried the joke to lighten her own anxiety and fear. And the new tension building inside her. A tension not helped by little touches, no matter how light they might be.

'Perhaps you've been working in Sumatra. You've been somewhere hot, from the look of your legs.'

'From the look of my legs? What have my legs got to do with anything?'

He hitched his trousers higher and peered down at the limbs in question.

'They're brown, but your feet are white. You've been wearing shorts and boots, though that's more likely to mean you're an outdoor worker here in Australia. Building worker, gardener, farmer.'

She saw more gleams of firelight on his teeth this time— a wider smile in the darkly bearded face.

'Boots and shorts, eh? Or perhaps just boots?' he said, ignoring her list of shorts-clad professions. 'Did you do any further investigations?'

He was fumbling with his belt, tugging at his zip.

Sam felt a flutter of something that should have been fear but wasn't. Perhaps because she knew she could easily evade him.

'Don't bother trying to impress me with whatever's tucked away in there,' she told him, talking so she didn't have to analyse what the flutter *might* have been. 'I'm a nurse, remember. I've seen more naked males than most women!'

'Well, that's a nice put-down,' he said, lifting his hands away to show her that both buckle and zip were still fastened. 'I was only teasing you. I'm tremendously grateful for all you've done. Heaven knows what would have become of me if you hadn't happened along.'

There was silence while he stirred the flames, then he turned and she could see his profile lit from behind. A neat, straight nose with a slight widening in the middle gave the profile great lines, and Sam suspected there was good bone structure behind that camouflage of beard. Strong, prominent cheek-bones above it.

'You did just happen along, didn't you?' he asked, and she heard the echo of despair—of the unremembered, the unfathomable—in the deep cadence of his voice.

'I did just happen along,' she assured him. 'I'm not Jocelyn, or anyone else you should remember. Now, let's forget about—'

'Forget things I can't remember?' he demanded harshly.

It was her turn to use touch. She rested her fingers lightly on his arm.

'Give it time,' she said. 'I know that sounds trite but it's all you can do.'

He covered her hand with his, and she felt the strength in his fingers. *And* the ripple effect of his touch.

There's no such thing as instant attraction.

And he's married!

'I should be thanking you, not growling at you.' His voice was low-toned, husky in the dusk. 'Do you think I might always be hard to get along with? That I might be a grouch by nature?'

Sam remembered those blue eyes, the gleam of white teeth, the electricity he sparked inside her.

'I doubt it,' she said, and heard her other self give a snort of silent laughter. You're judging a man by the ripples he starts in you? the inner cynic scoffed.

'Well, as my life's an all but total blank, we'll have to talk about you. Tell me about Sam.'

Again he interrupted her thoughts, and she shifted, kneeling to put another few sticks on the fire, not wanting to share details of her life with a stranger.

'The alternative's going to bed,' he added, 'and, although I'm not wearing a watch, I'm sure it's far too early.'

Going to bed?

Theoretically, sharing a hard bed with the stranger was the sensible thing to do, but what about the ripples?

The nonexistent but still disturbing instant attraction.

Not going to bed was an infinitely better idea.

'I'm a nurse. I live in Brisbane. Well, my home's out west, Goondiwindi, in fact, but I went to school and studied for my degree in Brisbane, and now I work there.'

She stopped, the mention of her home reminding her why she'd escaped to the rainforest for this break. Just thinking of the sprawling, prosperous town on the Queensland side of the river that marked, as the ranges did here, the state border, recalled the decision she had to make.

'That's it? That's your life history? Good grief, woman, I'm supposed to be the amnesiac around here!'

'It's a summary!' she said stiffly. 'All you need to know.'

'So when I write my thank-you-for-rescuing-me note, I send it to Sam, a nurse, in Brisbane.'

'T-Toowong! I live in T-Toowong.' She stuttered the

words at him, her composure betrayed by the thought of any future contact between them.

'Ah,' he responded gravely, 'that should help.'

There was silence for a moment, then, perhaps guessing she had no intention of telling him more, he said quietly, 'Maybe bed isn't such a bad option. My head's aching nearly as much as my ankle.'

'Oh, I'm sorry. I meant to give you more tablets.' Pleased to have something to do, Sam scrabbled for the first-aid kit. Of course he'd have a headache after tumbling down that cliff, she told herself, scooping water into a cup.

Then why hadn't he mentioned it earlier?

If a haematoma was building, it seemed logical that the pain would increase.

Should she keep him awake?

'And I've teabags. Would you like a cup of tea? And biscuits—fruit bars. They taste a bit like cardboard but they're very healthy.'

She was prattling on but couldn't seem to stop, her mouth accelerating in tandem with her panic. She handed him two tablets and the cup of water, then took their pannikins to the creek, scooped up more water and some sand, moving away to clean them so any remnants of their meal would be filtered through the stony ground before the water made its way back into the creek.

Having rinsed out the larger of the two pans, she filled it with clean water and was about to light the fire and set it to boil when Jack interrupted her mad burst of house-wifeliness.

'No tea for me, thanks,' he said.

'Do you feel sick? Nauseated? Is your headache local-ised? In the temples? One-sided?'

'Hey, calm down.'

Again his hand reached out and his fingers clasped her

arm. Barely touching—not in any way a threat—yet the ripples spread and her heart, already reacting to her mental jitters, lurched uneasily.

'I'm calm!'

The words were unnecessarily loud and they echoed eerily back to her.

Calm. Calm. Calm.

'No, you're not, you're panicking. My headache isn't bad and it isn't localised. It's the result of a bump on the head, not a subdural haematoma.'

'Subdural? I was thinking epidural,' Sam muttered. 'Now I've got something else to worry about.'

Then the implications of what he'd said struck her, and she looked up and caught him watching her.

'What do you know about subdural haematomas?' she asked, calming herself with the reminder that his ankle was definitely injured even if the memory loss was a sham.

'I don't know,' he replied, and the frustration in his voice told her it was the truth. 'Well, I do know. I know they can result from brain injury, when injured blood vessels leak blood into the space between the dura mater lining the skull and the spiderweb-like arachnoid layer over the brain. This puts pressure on the brain, and can cause long-term damage if not released. How's that, Nurse? Ten out of ten?'

'It's probably more than I could recite straight off, but if you've lived in places like the Sumatra, you probably needed more than basic first aid.'

Sam heard him chuckle.

'Not willing to concede I might have medical knowledge, are you, Sam from Toowong? Afraid I might steal your thunder? Undermine your authority on this little adventure? Don't you agree that if my brother's a brain surgeon, it's possible I might be a medical man?'

'*If* your brother's a brain surgeon?' Sam said dryly.

She remembered the feel of his fingers as they'd clasped her hand earlier and touched her arm. Not doctor's fingers at all. Farmer, gardener or a labourer of some kind seemed far more likely.

Not that it mattered what he did. After tomorrow—after she got him safely to a hospital—she'd never see him again.

The thought made her want to touch him, as if to reassure herself that this was really happening, but touching him was dangerous.

'I think you're right about getting some sleep. I want to get started at first light tomorrow.' She considered the logistics of settling down for the night, found her towel, put toothpaste on her brush then dropped the tube on the ground near her companion, filled a cup with water and excused herself.

'I'll go bush for my ablutions. You do whatever you have to do. I've left the toothpaste there. Then choose whichever side of the bed you want.'

'Toothpaste, huh? Is that a ''clean your teeth before you go to bed'' suggestion, or an indication that the night could hold some promise?'

'In your dreams, buster!' Sam snorted. 'I'm sharing my sleeping bag with you so you don't freeze to death, but we'll both have all our clothes on and the headache you've got now will be nothing to what you'll end up with if you start any funny business.'

His husky chuckle followed her into the darkness and she had to chide herself about feeling attraction to total strangers and remind herself that villains were just as likely to have a sense of humour as good guys.

By the time she returned, he was no more than a hump under the sleeping bag.

'I left the fire burning so you'd see the light but perhaps we should put it out,' the hump said.

'I'll see to it,' Sam told him, using the little light it shed to study the makeshift bed and work out how much room there was for her.

Shoving the little torch into her pocket, she poured water on the flames, then spread the ashes and scattered sand across them. The moon rose above the trees as she completed her task, shedding a silver light over their little campsite.

She sat tentatively on the very edge of the tent she'd spread to form a groundsheet, and pulled off her boots and wet socks. Her long trousers were still damp from the knees down, but as she'd used her single change of clothes to pad their 'mattress', she'd have to put up with that minor discomfort. Gingerly, she eased her body under the sleeping bag, keeping as much space as possible between herself and Jack.

'I could get up and find some stout sticks if you like. Put them down the middle to mark out our territories.'

His deep voice barely broke the stillness.

'I wouldn't have suggested sharing the bed if I didn't trust you,' Sam told him, hoping the coolness in her voice would stop any further conversation.

'Or if you hadn't known a swift kick to my ankle would completely immobilise me.'

Sam smiled in the darkness. As that very thought had crossed her mind, she couldn't argue. She breathed deeply instead and hoped that sleep would come.

'Although it would be warmer if we snuggled,' the wretch persisted.

'And put your ankle at risk? Not to mention your head if you happened to get fresh?'

'Not into snuggling up to strangers?'

'No! Now go to sleep!'

Sam hoped the words sounded less shrill to him than

they did to her, but she was beginning to realize that this hadn't been such a good idea. They didn't need to be snuggling for the body awareness he radiated to affect her skin. And no pile of sticks would be high enough to stop the waves of whatever it was he sent her way.

Was this what they called sex appeal?

Did he affect all women in a similar way?

Was this how his wife felt?

The memory of that band of gold around his ring finger jarred her and she rolled over on her side, turning her back to him, hoping to stop whatever it was.

Shouldn't that, alone, have stopped the attraction thing— which, of course, didn't exist?

Her thoughts dithered into a pre-sleep muddle, switching from practical to impossible, and back again.

She should have left him the sleeping bag and some food and pushed on to get help.

But what if he'd wandered? Lost consciousness?

Ha! That was something to take precedence over the transmissions of whatever it was. She pondered what might be happening inside his skull. And the possible consequences.

Should she let him sleep?

How could she tell when sleep lapsed into unconsciousness?

'My headache's better, thanks to the tablets. I don't believe the pain of a haematoma would have been eased by paracetamol.'

'Are you reading my mind?' she demanded, and heard him chuckle.

'No, but I could feel your tension from way over here on the far side of the moon. Relax, Sam, I'll be OK.'

But she couldn't relax when his mention of the pain relief had started another concern churning in her head.

'I shouldn't have given you paracetamol. I know it's not as bad as aspirin, but if you've a haemorrhage somewhere, you shouldn't have anything that might affect the clotting of your blood. Or fluids for that matter. You should be dehydrating in case there's an increase in intracranial pressure.'

She heard a rustle of bedclothes, then his hand rested lightly on her shoulder.

'I'm sure I'd know if there was anything sinister going on inside my head,' he said softly. 'Well, anything medically sinister!'

The last words had been intended as a joke, but Sam's worry meter slid skywards once again as her imagination took flight.

The man had no pack, no car keys, yet he'd somehow reached a very inaccessible spot then either fallen, jumped or been pushed.

Put sinister together with a limited medical knowledge and what did you get?

Drugs!

Dear heaven, she was out here in the wilderness, sharing her bed with a drug-dealer!

Would whoever didn't like him bother to make sure the job had been properly done? Had they heard her speak to him, call out, and realise they now had two people to eliminate?

A new sound made her tense. She held her breath, and tried to stop her rampaging thoughts. Then she heard the sound again, and smiled into the darkness as her body slowly relaxed.

Stuck in the wilderness with a drug-dealer who snored?

She propped herself onto one elbow and studied her sleeping companion. Her mother always rolled her father onto his side to stop the snoring, but Sam didn't want to hurt Jack's ankle, so she'd let him be. She worked out how he was lying, and where she'd have to aim her kick if he did happen to start anything.

Instinct told her it was unlikely. That the man was trustworthy. Her head scoffed at the idea. A trustworthy drug-dealer?

CHAPTER FOUR

A DULL throbbing pain—in his ankle, he realised—woke Jack, but opening his eyes to grey pre-dawn light, to tall trees crowding in around him, was the stuff of nightmares.

He remembered that he didn't know, that he couldn't remember.

He closed his eyes then opened them again. It wasn't a dream. Not that he'd thought it was. The place, the warm body curled so trustingly beside him, had already told him that.

Careful not to disturb said warm body, he turned so he could see her shape and form.

Stupid woman, allowing herself to sleep so soundly next to a stranger. Not that she wouldn't be exhausted. A little slip of a thing like her. Sam must be what? Five four, perhaps? And slim. Nothing of her, yet she'd held him upright as they'd struggled down that blasted creek, then inched him down the cliff beside the waterfall.

And she hadn't slept very well during the night. Several times she'd poked or prodded him, seeking a response, perhaps making sure his sleep hadn't turned into something more permanent.

Worrying about him.

He remembered the worry in her clear green eyes, the grim set of her lips—surely made for smiles—as she'd taken his weight. Then the feel of her body, not so slim where taut breasts had pressed against his shirt.

Get your mind above your belt! He hauled back on the straying thoughts and glanced over to where the water, paler than the other shadows, tumbled into a cool, deep pool.

The night air had been as cold as his rescuer had predicted, and a crispness lingered. But the pool beckoned, promising relief from internal heat. What he wouldn't do to plunge his aching, battered body into those green depths!

Perhaps they could swim before they headed off again. Buoyancy would take his weight so it wouldn't hurt his ankle.

Hmm.

He turned back to the sleeping woman. Well, to the cap of red-blonde curls which was all he could see of her. She was as game as Ned Kelly. Would her confidence extend to stripping off and plunging into the creek?

Somehow he doubted it. Down to underwear perhaps. For all her guts, she had a reserve about her that suggested modesty would insist on some covering.

He could feel his body stirring as licentious thoughts again flickered like moths in his head. Plenty of room for moth-like thoughts. The stuff that should be filling all his brain cells was still missing.

And remembering not remembering made frustration swell within him. He shifted carefully away from his slumbering companion, slid out from under her sleeping bag and, using his scrabbling-along-on-his-backside mode of travel, inched towards the sheltering forest.

Sam awoke to find herself alone although she could have sworn there'd been the warmth of another body close to hers not long ago.

She remembered Jack and the drama of the previous day. She sat up and looked around.

'Hey! Where are you?'

'In the bathroom,' came the deep reply. 'Did you think I'd sprouted wings and flown away?'

As he spoke she heard a shuffling and saw him reappear, easing himself back towards her, arms and one leg helping the progress.

'I've been looking at that pool. Do we have time for a quick dip before we head off again?'

Sam turned from her contemplation of the bearded stranger to study the pool and the surrounding rocks. Access was easy enough and she guessed he'd be able to get out again one-legged. And she was certainly sticky and uncomfortable enough for a swim to be a real treat.

Forget it! she told herself.

Stripping off to swim alone in the pristine water was one thing, but stripping down to underwear and swimming with a stranger was a very different kettle of fish.

However, there was an alternative that had appeal. Given how, in spite of instant attraction not existing, the man affected her, even in the sober light of early morning.

'I've been wondering about the best way to get us out of here. Why don't you stay and swim, then, keeping to the creek bank, you can begin to work your way along it, taking your time and resting when the pain's too bad, while I go on ahead and get help?'

Jack was close enough by now for her to see his face clearly, and she'd watched him as she'd spoken, half expecting him to protest against this plan. But what she hadn't expected was the look of bleak despair in his eyes.

'Will it make so much difference? Save so much time? I mean, once you get to wherever you have to go, you'll have to contact emergency services. Presumably they'll have to rally around, call in their volunteers, and then get back here to me. Wasted resources, surely, when, with help, I could get out on my own?'

His voice was calm and matter-of-fact enough to make the suggestion sound logical, but Sam, having seen his eyes, guessed at the dark forces seething in his head. To be faced with not knowing who you were was one thing, but to be alone with that knowledge…

Unwilling to traumatise him further, she fell in with his plan.

'But we won't swim,' she told him firmly. 'The sooner we can get you to a doctor, the better.'

She grabbed her backpack, shifted off the 'mattress' she'd contrived, and began to tuck things carefully back into place.

'Have a drink of water, and some dried fruit. The container's over there. It's after six now, we'll stop for a cup of tea and a more substantial snack at eight. Does that suit you?'

She glanced up but avoided his eyes this time, noticing instead the way his hair fell forward at the side of his face—imagining it drawn back in a short ponytail, revealing the strength of those sharp cheekbones.

'You're the boss,' he said easily, reaching her side and picking up the sleeping bag, then rolling it into a tight sausage shape. 'Got a bag for this?'

She passed it to him, careful to avoid skin on skin contact in case the vibrations started up again.

Not that they'd ever really stopped.

'Hey, we've slept together,' he protested, when he did brush his hand across her wrist and she reared back like a frightened rabbit. 'Curled up against me like a sleeping baby, you were, and soon I'll be draped like a very heavy scarf around your shoulders, so stop the skittering routine every time I touch you. It's accidental, that's all!'

'I'm not reacting to you, I just don't like being touched!' Sam retorted. 'Even accidentally!'

She moved away, but not so far she didn't hear him murmur, 'Now, why don't I believe that story?'

Furious with herself, Sam thrust the rest of the gear any-how into the pack. She wanted to get away from him. She should have insisted she go on ahead, not listened to the man or been swayed by a bleakness in his so-expressive eyes.

'Have you got your stick?' she asked, swinging the pack onto her back to show she meant business.

'I thought we were to feast on the dried fruit and clear mountain water before we departed,' he reminded her, and she dropped her burden back to the ground and sighed.

'And I need a wash,' she admitted. 'Damn! I've packed my toothbrush.'

'But you forgot the toothpaste,' Jack told her, grinning at her as he held up the tube. 'Be like me and use your finger.'

She scowled in case he thought he could get around her with his smiles, and headed for the bush. Far enough in to be out of sight, but not far enough to release her frustration with a loud yell or a stream of curses.

Did she know enough curses to make a stream of them? Probably not!

The answer left her even more dejected!

Back at the creek, Sam splashed cold water across her face and neck, moved away to wipe toothpaste over her teeth, rinsed her mouth, then grabbed a handful of apricots and dates from the container Jack held up towards her.

'Now let's go!' she muttered at him. 'Can you stow that and the cup in one of your pockets? It's probably easier for you to use the cup to drink than to squat down by the creek. Although it's cool, you need to keep your fluids up.'

Her thoughts fluttered back to head injuries and pressure. Shouldn't she be decreasing his fluids? Wasn't that why head-injured patients were given diuretics?

'Damn!'

'Was it something I did?'

She realised she'd let the word escape and chuckled at the tentative query.

'Not this time,' she assured Jack. 'I was simply regretting not taking more notice of my lectures in emergency medicine. I'd foolishly decided, early in my course, that I wanted to work in Theatre, and although I had to do prac. work in every department, most of what I learned went into my head and straight back out again.'

She dropped down beside him, easing herself into position by his side.

'Never mind! Here we go again. We'll stand up first and I'll give you time to get your balance before we move off.'

He put his arm around her shoulders and she registered the faint pleasure of familiarity. Then she banned the thought and concentrated on getting him upright.

'I should be able to put more weight on my foot, now it's splinted,' Jack said, and, knowing he'd insist on trying, Sam waited—and watched.

Saw the colour leach from his skin as his tentative attempt failed.

'Not to worry,' she said quickly. 'We managed yesterday and we'll do it again today. We can take our time and still be out by nightfall.'

'Nightfall? How far do you go in these solitary rambles? Isn't it irresponsible to come in here on your own?'

'To answer your questions in order,' Sam began as they moved off in their awkward tandem, 'I work on time, not distance. I usually come for two days. One day in, and one day out. Normally I'd have camped by the waterfall but yesterday I'd made good time so I decided to go further. And as for irresponsible, my brothers know where I am, and when to expect a phone call to say I'm back at the car.

Believe me, if they don't hear by the designated time, they'll have the search parties out immediately.'

She felt his body tense—a strange reaction to such an inoffensive conversation.

'If you've a mobile phone why didn't you phone for help yesterday?' he demanded angrily, leaning away as far as he could from her as if he wanted to distance himself from her perfidy.

Sam waved her free hand towards tree-clad mountains that hemmed them in on all sides.

'No signal! There's only a faint one from the car. Believe me, if I could have got help to you yesterday, I would have.'

Which possibly wasn't the best thing she could have said, for it killed all conversation between them for half an hour.

And though Sam had tried to find a neutral subject, because talking kept her mind off their snail-like progress, it was Jack who broke the silence in the end.

'Brothers? In Goondiwindi, or the other place? What did you call it?'

'Toowong.' Sam answered automatically, her brain trying to wade through its own forgetfulness. Was forgetting things post-trauma a sign he was deteriorating? Though, realistically, there was no reason why he should remember the suburb she'd mentioned only once.

'And brothers? Plural? Is there a tribe of them?'

She forgot forgetting and smiled.

'Only two. Twins. Identical. Absolute terrors, both of them, but since they came to live in Brisbane to go to university, they've taken on a kind of joint custodial role, checking out any man I might happen to meet, the time I get home. Far worse than Mum ever was, even when I was a teenager.'

'And are they always home to check out your arrival? How old are they? The university students I knew weren't noted for keeping early hours, or even great reliability as far as time was concerned.'

He stopped and she had to stop with him.

'How can I possibly know something like that when I can't remember my own name?' he demanded.

Sam shrugged and felt the movement of his arm on her shoulders.

'I doubt if anyone can explain amnesia—not fully,' she told him. 'But I do know memory usually returns. You might end up with a few gaps here or there but, when you think about it, who needs to keep all the memories we must amass?'

'Good point,' he agreed, swinging forward at the same time, indicating, perhaps, that the conversation was at an end.

'And what are they studying, these brothers of yours?'

'Peter's doing chemistry—well, science with a chemistry major—and Sean's into IT.'

'IT?' Jack repeated the two letters. Made a word of it. 'It?'

'Information technology. He's a computer nerd.'

'Five-eight, skinny, thick glasses?'

'Six-one, rugby player, twenty-twenty vision.'

Sam felt Jack's chest move as he chuckled, and felt an unexpected surge of pleasure that she could make him laugh.

There's no such thing as instant attraction, she reminded herself. And even if there was, you're not the kind of girl who falls for married men!

'They both play rugby,' she added, and talking about the twins kept them going until she called a halt.

While the kettle boiled and Jack rested, she surreptitiously studied her map, trying to work out how far they'd come. And how long the rest of the journey would take!

'Phone your brothers and get them to send an ambulance to meet us,' Jack insisted when, as dusk again bathed the countryside in softer light, they finally reached Sam's car. 'You're too exhausted to drive anywhere.'

'I'll phone the boys but I'm not too tired to drive. I can have you in Beaudesert Hospital almost before the ambulance has time to leave its base.'

She read the mutiny in his eyes.

'Just get in the car!' she told him. 'I'm OK to drive but far too tired to argue with a stubborn mule.'

Mentally and physically exhausted, she slumped behind the wheel, and took a deep breath to summon whatever poor reserves of strength might yet remain. Her patient had survived the day, which made the serious things like haematomas seem unlikely.

Considering the pain he must have been in throughout their awkward trek, he had considerable reserves of physical resiliency himself. In fact, he had guts and courage and a tenacity that left her awed. Mental toughness, too, to put aside the nagging doubts of memory loss.

The only problem was the bond that Sam had felt developing between them. Unwanted, unnecessary, but undeniable.

Although there was no such thing as instant attraction.

And he was married.

Propinquity, that's all it had been. Once she dropped him at the hospital, that was it.

They'd never see each other again.

'So, shall we go?'

She turned towards him and found a small smile to offer.

'You did very well, getting out of there,' she told him.

'Now she admits it!' he said, raising his hands and rolling his eyes heavenwards. 'Nag, nag, nag all day, and now she tells me I did well!'

He touched her lightly on the shoulder to soften the teasing words, and added softly, 'I wouldn't have made it without you. Thank you, Sam.'

The heartfelt words made Sam's eyes water.

'Don't thank me yet,' she said with a gruff nonchalance. 'You still have to survive my driving! According to the twins, all women drivers should be banned. And in case it's in your memory blanks, not memory banks, I gather that's a common male opinion.'

She started the engine, checked he had his seat belt on, then carefully eased the car into reverse. Great! No grinding of gears, no fumbling with the gear lever. She lifted her foot off the clutch and went forward into the trunk of the tree beneath which she'd parked.

Cheeks aflame with humiliation, she tried again and stalled.

'Oops! I'm not usually this bad. Just tired.'

But in her heart she knew it was more than tiredness. Her mind, usually neat and orderly, was a jumble of emotions. Fatigue definitely came into it, and awareness of her companion in the car, but overlying all was a sense of loss that soon, too soon, they'd be parting. Jack to a bed in a hospital ward, his amnesia someone else's problem. While she'd go home and, in another day, return to work.

In another two days she'd have Henry arriving on her doorstep. Expecting a decision. A decision she thought she'd made, until....

'Damn!'

'I expect you've flooded it,' Jack said, and she was glad he thought her lack of success behind the wheel had caused the swearing.

'I expect I have,' she muttered. 'There!'

The engine caught, she found reverse and they moved off, in the correct direction this time. She backed up, turned the wheel, changed to first and started carefully down the slope towards the gravel road.

A chance-met stranger, that's all he is, she told herself as she tried to concentrate most of her attention on the narrow, winding road. And married, remember, for all he mutters 'pigs' each time you bring it up.

He's nothing to you and never will be.

'Where's this Beaudesert place you mention?'

His question registered but failed to distract her.

'Just down the road.'

You'll never see him again.

'I realise it's just down the road, but which road? You talked about the state border. Which side are we on? Which state are we in?'

This time his questions were sufficiently bizarre for her to forget her mental misery.

She frowned as she tried to put herself in his shoes.

'I simply can't imagine what it must be like,' she said. 'Not remembering enough to anchor yourself in the present—in a particular place. We're in Queensland. Beaudesert is a town about fifty miles south of Brisbane. Big enough to have a hospital, which you'll need to get your ankle set.'

'Then you'll go on to Brisbane?'

The bleakness she'd seen in his eyes earlier now echoed in his voice.

'Well, you'll have nurses, doctors and cute radiographers to take care of you so there'll be no need for me to hang around.'

'Cute radiographers?'

She nodded and said firmly, 'Radiographers are always cute!' No way was she going to start feeling sorry for him!

There was silence for a moment, then he said, 'You didn't phone your brothers.'

Sam glanced at the clock on the dash.

'I've another half an hour. We'll be in town by then.'

She drove on, ignoring the mental suggestions her fertile mind was flinging at her. Like he'd get better treatment at a Brisbane hospital. And neurology specialists who could explain his amnesia and reassure him about the outcome.

It's not your place to worry over him!

The emergency department at the sprawling country hospital was quiet. In fact, if the solicitude that greeted them—orderlies with a wheelchair, nurses fluttering anxiously—was any guide, they were pleased to have a patient to break the boredom.

One of the fluttering nurses collared Sam.

'Could you give me his details while they take him across to X-Ray?'

Sam shrugged.

'I can't tell you much, although I suppose I know as much as he does. I found him in the bush.'

The nurse, whose badge introduced her as Robyn, chuckled.

'And he followed you home?'

'It's no laughing matter. He'd fallen down a cliff. No backpack, although that could have been left at the top, no identification on him, and he doesn't remember anything.'

'So, what's his name?' Robyn asked, pen poised above her admission chart.

'He doesn't know,' Sam repeated patiently, although she was once again realising how frustrating it must be for Jack. 'He can't remember who he is or why he was where he was or how he got there or anything. We decided to call him Jack if that's any help.'

'Who's "we"?' Robyn demanded, and Sam heard suspicion creeping into the woman's voice.

'He and I. I couldn't call him "hey, you" for a day and a half.'

'You've been lugging him around in the bush for a day and a half?'

The nurse didn't wait for a reply, but whisked away, disappearing into what Sam assumed was a superior's office.

I should go. Right now, Sam decided as intuition suggested there was more trouble looming. But it felt wrong to disappear without saying goodbye to Jack. Without at least hearing how badly he'd injured his ankle.

She sat down on a chair against the wall of the big waiting room and closed her eyes. The sensation of falling jerked her awake.

Less complicated if you go now, the inner voice murmured. Less fuss.

How long had she been asleep?

She peered down the corridor—no sign of Jack's entourage returning—no sign of Robyn, the nurse who'd wanted 'details', then disappeared. Go now, the inner voice repeated, and Sam, tempted, glanced towards the door.

It wheezed asthmatically open as she watched and a policeman who looked younger than her brothers came striding in. He obviously knew his way around for he, too, headed for the office Robyn had entered, reappearing seconds later with the nurse in tow and heading straight towards Sam.

Too late to make a run for it now!

'So you're the one who found this man. What's your name, miss?'

Sam dutifully supplied her name, address and the sketchy details of Jack's advent into her life. She kept the 'my brother's a brain surgeon' to herself, feeling Jack could tell the policeman that titbit.

'So you went up the creek alone?' the policeman said when she'd finished.

'Yes.'

'Bit unusual, that!' Suspicion was crusted on each word.

He'd stopped writing but still had the notebook in his hand, as if he expected more information to jot down on its pages.

'Not for me, it's not,' Sam said firmly. 'I work in a stressful job, live in a madhouse where there could be anything from four to fourteen staying overnight, and sometimes when I'm off duty I like to get right away from people.'

Sam read the disbelief in his face and wondered, as he began to scribble, what he felt compelled to write. Possibly her flippant use of 'madhouse' to describe her Brisbane home.

'And you say you found this fellow? Stumbled over him, as it were?'

'I didn't stumble over him. He fell. Right in front of me.'

'Bit lucky, that! Think of all the places he could have fallen, yet he happened to fall right in front of you.'

A queasy feeling stirred in the pit of Sam's stomach, and she stared at the young policeman in disbelief.

'Do you think I planned this?' she demanded. 'Planned to ruin my days off by helping an injured man out of the bush? Or do you think I injured him? That I hit him on the head, pushed him down a cliff, broke his ankle, then helped him out?'

'You could have left him there. Gone for help,' the policeman pointed out.

'I considered it,' Sam retorted, 'but I'm a nurse, and I know how disorientated head-injured patients can become.

If I'd left him there he could have wandered off, got lost or injured himself more badly. Do you think it was any fun, lugging that great hulking brute out of there?'

No reply, although as the policeman turned away, bending to speak to Robyn in an undertone, Sam thought she heard the word 'guilty', and the queasiness in her stomach turned to ice.

More than anything, she wanted to get away from this place, to return to the security and normal chaos of her home. No one had said she couldn't leave, but as she stood up, intending, this time, to go, the sound of voices echoing along the corridor made her pause.

Jack was still in the wheelchair, but this time his ankle was plastered, the dark blue cast propped out in front of him as two laughing nurses wheeled him back towards the emergency waiting room.

Sam shook her head. Either she was so tired she was missing bits of time, or the policeman's questions had taken longer than she'd imagined. No way she could escape without a goodbye now.

'Here he is,' one of the nurse escort said cheerfully. 'He's got pain relief, his X-rays and instructions about when to see a local doctor. It's all written down so he doesn't forget.'

The other nurse chuckled at what was obviously a joke between them but Sam failed to see anything funny in the situation.

'What do you mean, "Here he is"?' she demanded. 'He's not mine!'

She regretted her own vehemence when she saw a flash of pain in Jack's eyes, but the nurse had missed any subtle nuances. She was following her own agenda.

'Well, he has to go somewhere,' she said. 'We don't keep broken ankles in hospital these days.'

'But what about his head injury? His amnesia?' Sam could hear the pitch of her voice rising. Great! A bout of hysterics would convince the policeman she was mad!

'We've X-rayed his head. It's all clear. Although there's a bump on the back of it that suggests he was struck or struck it on something. Lucky for him he's got a thick skull. And the doctor says his memory will come back. Possibly within another day or two, given that the head injury was mild rather than severe.'

She might as well have been speaking Swahili for all the sense Sam was making of the words. Their abandonment of the man seemed unbelievable.

'B-but he doesn't know who he is,' she stammered. 'You can't turn him out on the streets. Not with a broken ankle.'

'Certainly not with a broken ankle,' Jack put in, and Sam was forced to look his way—something she'd been avoiding since she'd seen that flash of pain earlier.

'You know what I mean!' she grouched. 'There must be something you do with people like him. Somewhere for them to go.'

'Perhaps a police cell,' the patient said cheerfully, and Sam's temper snapped.

'Stop making a joke of this!' she stormed. 'Don't you realise the seriousness of this situation? How on earth are you going to look after yourself? You've got no name, no money, no access to anything. What do you think you're going to do?'

'Well, the hospital has said they'll lend me crutches, provided I give them back when the ankle's healed, and I thought perhaps busking...'

Sam scowled at him, but turned to the policeman.

'You must know what to do,' she said. 'He can't be the first person in the world who's landed in hospital, not knowing who he is.'

'First I know of in Beaudesert,' the policeman said. He scratched his head. 'I suppose there's always the Sallies. Or one of the other church groups. I guess I could make some phone calls.'

An image of the injured man, lost and alone among equally lost and homeless men, rose up in Sam's mind.

'Don't bother!' she snapped at the policeman. 'I'll take him home with me. You've got my address. You do whatever you have to do about registering him as a missing person, and let me know as soon as you find someone to claim him.'

'But he's not missing—he's here,' one of the nurses said.

Sam bit her tongue to prevent a real outburst, swept the woman aside and grabbed the handles of the wheelchair.

'And not one word out of you!' she growled as she pushed the patient towards the door, an agitated nurse following close behind.

'But—'

'Don't tempt me,' Sam warned again as the doors wheezed open once again.

'You've forgotten these. They're adjustable.'

Another nurse came hurrying after them, a pair of metal crutches in her hands.

'That's what I was trying to tell you,' Jack said, taking the crutches and laying them across his lap, which already held an X-ray envelope. Both nurses halted by the door. Because their jurisdiction ended there, or did they fear Sam's temper?

Jack was silent for all of sixty seconds as Sam pushed the chair across the paved parking area, then, as they approached the car, he asked, 'What's got you in such a snit? I can understand you didn't want to be landed with a stranger, but you were ready to blow a fuse before I reappeared on the scene. Policeman upset you?'

'You might say that!' Sam growled, abandoning the chair while she unlocked the car and opened the passenger-side door. 'He seems to think you're the victim of spousal abuse. That I lured you into the rainforest, hit you on the head, pushed you down a cliff, then in a fit of either guilt or remorse opted to drag you back out again.'

'I must admit it did cross my mind at one point,' Jack said.

'If it *had* been me,' Sam told him in no uncertain terms, 'I'd have left you there!'

His reaction to this piece of spite started as a chuckle but built to full-throated laughter, as joyous a sound as Sam had ever heard.

But she didn't want to be diverted by delightful laughter, she wanted to stay cross.

Cross was better than attraction.

'It's no joke!' she snapped at him. 'And bear in mind I can still abandon you. If you know what's good for you, you'll get yourself into the car and stay quiet for the entire journey to Brisbane.'

He did more than that. He fell asleep, and Sam felt guilty that she'd berated him when he was obviously in so much distress.

She enjoyed the quiet, familiar drive through the darkness, but when they reached the outskirts of Brisbane and began passing under streetlights, she slowed, took her time and turned from time to time to study the man who slept so trustingly beside her.

Was he special in some way, that she'd reacted to him?

Not with that beard all but obscuring his face!

Although it *was* a nice face. With his hair trimmed so you saw the high, wide forehead, with its neat crescents of solid-looking eyebrows. And with the beard at least trimmed—no, she'd prefer it shaved right off. She was fairly certain there was a clean, firm jawline beneath the fuzz!

And with his beard removed, you'd see more of the lips that tantalised her with little smiles. Lips that, even half-concealed, were full and very shapely.

Forget him. He's married.

There's no such thing as instant attraction!

She stopped looking, concentrating on getting them both home alive, then as she pulled into the drive of the big house the family all considered their Brisbane home, she felt a wave of uncertainty so strong she wondered if dropping him off at a local church shelter might not be the best option.

'Hey, sis! Where's the man?'

It was Sean who bolted down the steps towards her as she stepped out of the car.

'What do you mean, where's the man?' she asked, already regretting she'd mentioned her adventure on the phone.

He shrugged and smiled at her.

'You're not telling me you left the poor chap in hospital in Beaudesert? Abandoned him completely? Not when Pete and I have spent the last hour devising a game of "Find your Memory" for him.'

'It's not a joke, Sean!' she told her irrepressible brother. 'Certainly not for him.' Then she weakened, and added, 'He's in the car. And although it will be difficult to get him up the steps the first time, he'll be better off upstairs. That way he won't have to tackle the steps in order to get fed.'

She considered the logistics of getting Jack up the angled steps to the wide, iron-laced verandah.

'Give Pete a call. With both of you to help he won't have to put any weight on his new plaster.'

She walked around the car and opened the door, then reached in and shook her passenger's shoulder.

'Wake up,' she said gently. 'We're home.'

And in the bright light that flooded the driveway at night, she saw his blue eyes widen, as if in alarm, and then the expression turn to warmth as he repeated what she'd said.

'We're home?'

Fortunately, the twins arrived before she had time to consider her reaction to those words.

'Here comes the cavalry,' Pete rumbled. 'So, Mr Noname, what do you want with our sister? We assume your intentions are honourable, injured sir. And that you'll respect the rules and regulations of the Abbots' house during your sojourn with us.'

Bewildered blue eyes turned to Sam.

'They're both mad,' she said gently. 'After twenty-four hours you'll probably regret not opting for the Sallies.'

'Nonsense, he'll learn to love us and hope his memory never returns so he can stay with us for ever,' Sean insisted. 'But our immediate problem, mate, is to get you out of there and up the stairs. They built the houses big in the old days, but disabled access was an unheard-of luxury.'

He was peering into the car as he spoke, and had shaken Jack's hand somewhere in the conversation.

'Will you trust the two of us to lift you or are you better on your own one foot with us as human crutches?'

'I'll get out first,' Jack replied. 'Good foot steady, then take my weight on the door and see how things look.'

'That means he's likely to keel over when he stands up,' Sam told her brothers. 'He's more badly injured than he lets on, for all the lack of evidence.'

'Well, the man's come tumbling down a cliff—of course he's badly injured.'

Pete had joined Sean by the car and Sam, realizing that

beneath their banter they had the situation well in hand, retrieved the crutches from the back seat, then opened the boot to get her pack.

An hour later, with the help of the twins, Jack had been bathed, fed and tucked into bed. The painkillers he'd been given earlier while his ankle had been set must have kicked in again, for when Sam looked in to check on him he was sound asleep.

Weary herself, yet too hyped up to sleep, she headed for the kitchen to heat some milk for cocoa.

'You realise he's married, sis,' Pete said, coming in behind her and propping himself on the big table that dominated the family's favourite room.

Sam turned to see Sean arrive, an identical expression of concern on his face.

'I've got eyes! I could see his ring. What are you suggesting? That I should only offer help to single men? That I should have left him there in the bush to die? You're as bad as that bloody policeman!'

'What policeman?' They chorused the question.

'In Beaudesert. His favoured scenario was spousal abuse!'

The twins chortled their delight, and immediately began propounding riotous scenarios of Sam belabouring the poor man with everything from brooms to frying pans.

Sam decided maybe cocoa wasn't such a good idea. She'd head to bed now! While they were distracted by their stupid jokes.

Before they took the subject any further.

And if, for some unfathomable reason, it hurt her to think about that gold band, well, that was for her to know—and the twins not to find out!

CHAPTER FIVE

SAM woke late, having forgotten to set the alarm. And, strangely enough, she hadn't been disturbed by the usual departure noises from the twins.

Because they hadn't departed, she found when she wandered, bleary-eyed and heavy-limbed, into the kitchen in search of coffee to help her wake up.

They were sitting at the kitchen table, one on either side of Jack, who was looking very comfortably ensconced in *her* chair.

The thought of how she must look—tousled hair, sleep-creased skin—made her want to bolt back to her bedroom and start the day again, but the boys were already greeting her, Jack swinging to face her, smiling at her.

'I'm a Garfield fan myself,' he said, and Sam looked down at the faded cotton Garfield T-shirt she'd worn to bed. Somehow it seemed shorter than she remembered it, more revealing of her legs. Legs that were prickling with their bareness.

'I thought you'd still be sleeping,' she said, feeling embarrassed. 'I'll go and change.' She turned, then remembered her manners and faced him again. 'How are you feeling today? Did you sleep well?'

Guilt that if he hadn't slept well she'd not have known curled in her stomach. Some nurse she'd turned out to be!

'I slept extremely well, and in case your interest in my welfare extends to nourishment, the twins have also fed and watered me.'

'And lent you clothes,' Sean added.

'Even clean jocks,' Pete put in. 'Greater love hath no man, et cetera, than to part with his jocks for an amnesiac intruder.'

'Now we're working on the memory game with him. Trying to help him remember.'

Used to the twins' banter, Sam turned her attention to their guest.

'I don't suppose you'd do me another good turn and rescue me from them?' he said plaintively. 'I realise your parents couldn't tell how they'd turn out, back when they were born—'

'Or they'd have abandoned them at birth?' Sam smiled at Jack. 'They are a little tiring at times, but they mean well.'

'And to think we've been so helpful,' Sean protested. 'He's already remembered his brother's a brain surgeon and he knows someone called Jocelyn, so all we have to do is phone that radio station that broadcasts the lost-and-found animals programme and list him with them.'

'Problem is,' Pete expounded, 'you usually have to put a name—like "answers to Snookums"—and Jack here hasn't got a clue.'

Sam left them to their teasing, hurrying back to her bedroom, needing, even more than to get dressed, some time to consider the consequences of bringing this man home.

The boys might be joking, but they'd obviously accepted him as easily as they would have a stray dog. Only you couldn't have a man put down if he proved to be too much to handle.

'I think you should phone the local police and report him found,' Pete announced, when she returned to the kitchen in jeans and a baggy T-shirt she'd stolen from one of her brothers. 'Maybe Beaudesert isn't up to speed with their computers and his description hasn't been circulated.

Actually, there's a cute new blonde working at the local station. She might come up to interview him.'

'Don't you mind the sexist twaddle these two carry on with?' Jack asked her, the smile she found so disconcerting agleam in his eyes.

'They know I'd biff them if I thought for one minute they were serious,' Sam assured him. 'And speaking of two—where's the echo?'

'Right here!'

Sean walked in with a sheaf of paper in his hand. He waved them at Jack.

'I've been looking your condition up on the net.'

Jack turned a questioning glance towards Sam.

'Internet. Computer nerd, remember.'

He smiled at her explanation and she decided that sitting down might be better than making coffee. She sank into Gran's chair at the far end of the table.

He's married and you don't believe in instant attraction. Although she was beginning to disbelieve the second part of that reminder.

'Would you make me a coffee while Sean explains?' she asked Pete.

And as one twin got up to do her bidding, the other began explaining what he'd found out about amnesia.

'I'd say you've got the Swiss cheese type of loss,' he began, and as his audience chortled he gave them all a stern glare and added, 'That might not sound scientific but it's how a learned professor described it. Holes in your memory as random as the holes in Swiss cheese.'

Jack rubbed his forehead.

'It's a perfect fit as far as I'm concerned,' he admitted.

Sam was glad the length of the table lay between them so there was no way she could touch his arm to offer comfort.

'I thought it might,' Sean agreed. 'The other interesting thing is how long memory loss might last. Here's where you don't seem to fit, given that you appear to be operating normally. Walking—as best you can—talking, knowing things about your likes and dislikes. Apparently the length of time you are likely to suffer amnesia is in direct relation to the severity of the head injury.'

'In what way?' Sam nodded her thanks to Pete as he placed her coffee on the table, but her attention was on Sean's words.

'Well, according to a test that's called GOAT—' ribald laughter greeted this acronym '—which stands,' Sean continued with dignity, 'for Galveston Orientation and Amnesia Test, with minor head injury you can lose your memory for less than five minutes. Five to sixty minutes is rated as mild. Sixty minutes to twenty-four hours is considered moderate, twenty-four hours to seven days severe, while more than seven days is extremely severe.'

Sam watched their guest to see how he was reacting to this information, and saw the frown draw creases in his forehead.

'But which comes first?' he asked Sean. 'If my amnesia lasts five days, is the head injury then classified as severe, or do they find the crack in my skull and say, "Hey, this is severe, the man won't know himself for seven days"?'

Sean flicked through his papers.

'Nothing here to answer that, but I know plenty of footballers who've had mild to moderate concussion, and while they might never get to remember exactly what happened during that particular scrum or ruck, they didn't forget who they were.'

'Initially they might have,' Pete reminded him. 'The five-minute, minor classification. Remember how the coach always asks you who you are after an injury, and usually what day it is as well.'

'Stupid question,' Sean grumbled. 'When we mostly play Sundays so it's a safe bet.'

He was still perusing his papers.

'There's something else here. About the GOAT thing being less reliable when focal cortical contusions are present. That make any sense to you, Sammie?'

'Well, the cortex is the outer layer of a body organ like the brain, rather than an inner layer. Focal's what it seems—the focal part. Contusions—bruising.'

'So he's bumped the outside of his brain,' Pete expounded, 'presumably against his skull as he came tumbling down the hill. Hey, sis, that was a great choice of names. Jack and Jill, remember? Jack came tumbling down—'

The 'Jack' in question gripped his forehead in both hands, and groaned theatrically. 'I don't suppose there's a nice Salvation Army shelter nearby? Or you'd know of a quiet lunatic asylum you could take me to? It would have to be better than listening to Bib and Bub's pathetic jokes.'

'Well, that's gratitude for you,' Sean complained. 'I think this is where we take back our clothes, bro.'

They advanced on their hapless guest, and it was only Sam's intervention, and her demands to know why they weren't at lectures, that eventually got them out of the room.

'I'm sorry,' she said, when they'd departed. 'They're hard enough to take when you're feeling one hundred per cent fit! How they must seem to someone not on top of things...'

'Nice lads, though,' Jack said, and Sam smiled.

'They are, that, although I don't know if "lads" is the

right word. Makes you sound like a grandfather, when you can't be that much older than them.'

'And how would you know that, Sleuth Sam?'

'Just looking at you. No grey in your hair, not much in your beard.'

'I've got grey in my beard?' He sounded so horrified Sam chuckled.

He rubbed his hand across the verdant growth, then felt the stitches she'd put in.

'It doesn't feel right, the beard,' he said. 'And now you've spoiled the symmetry of it when you patched my chin, I guess I could take it all off.'

Sam's heart wavered. Try as she might, she couldn't deny she found him attractive, but she'd always found the idea of kissing a bearded man very off-putting, so while he kept the beard her fantasies had limits. As far as she was concerned, the longer he kept it, the better.

'How old would you say I am?'

The question forced her to look at him, and again the uncertainty of not knowing was reflected in his eyes.

'Early thirties.'

Sam answered quickly, hoping a practical approach would kill off her emotional responses.

'And you? How old are you?'

She hesitated, then told herself it was normal enough conversation between chance-met acquaintances.

'Twenty-seven.'

'Seven years between you and the twins?'

Sam grinned at him.

'They were IVF babies—you should thank your lucky stars they aren't triplets! Back in the early days, a number of fertilised eggs were always implanted in the woman's womb and multiple births were common.'

He nodded.

'I seem to know that.'

'It probably comes more into the field of common knowledge than specialist knowledge, when you consider the amount of news coverage IVF gets.'

His smile appeared, peeking through the woolly undergrowth like a shy forest creature.

'I can't argue, can I, given how little I remember of anything?'

And given how she was responding to fugitive smiles, it was high time she distanced herself from this man.

'I think Pete was right about a visit to the local police. Not that they're local any more, but there's a station a couple of suburbs away. We could drive over there and ask if anyone's reported you missing.'

She frowned as something she'd read or heard sounded a faint chime in her head.

'I wonder how long you've been missing?' she said. 'In TV programmes, the police don't list an adult as missing until he or she's been gone forty-eight hours. If you told someone you'd be away a week and fell on your first day of walking, you won't have been reported and won't be showing up on any lists.'

'So we scrub the police?'

Sam considered this, but not for long.

'No. A report might come in from some other source. Perhaps someone's found your car.'

'If I had a car.'

Jack was sounding lost again, and Sam used practicality to boost his wavering confidence.

'You had to get to where you were. OK, so you walked into the rainforest, but you didn't walk to the park boundaries. Whichever way you came in, you had transport. Besides, taking you for a drive is a good idea. It will give you a chance to see if anything looks familiar.'

He didn't reply, but turned to retrieve the crutches which were leaning against the back of his chair.

'I'm getting the hang of this,' he said, standing up and distributing his weight between the two metal supports. 'Watch!'

He swung forward, moved the aids, swung again, then fell flat on his face, cursing and swearing while the yowling cat that had caused the accident fled the scene.

'Funny how that vocabulary wasn't in one of the holes of your memory,' Sam said, hurrying to his assistance.

But when she touched his arm, the attraction she was trying not to feel flooded through her body.

And through his, if the strange glow in his eyes was any indication.

'Damn cat!' he said huskily, and Sam knew the cat was the last thing on his mind.

'I should banish her from the house while you're here,' she suggested, still on her knees beside him, her fingers clamped to his arm as if held there by a magnetic force.

The air between them trembled with a tension that had nothing to do with cats, and Sam forgot all the reasons she shouldn't be attracted to this man and moved her hand, brushing it lightly across his skin, feeling the thick rope of muscle beneath it, and the hardness of bone.

'Don't banish the cat on my account,' he whispered, and Sam's heart reacted to the statement with a little leap more in keeping with words of love than practicality.

Or was it the look in his eyes, the deeper blueness, which had triggered the reaction in her heart?

'You should buy her one of those cat posts cats rub themselves against.'

The prosaic suggestion interrupted Sam's mental analysis of the situation—and brought her back to reality with a thud.

'Anything to ensure your comfort,' she managed to retort, then felt guilty when she saw her guest's cheeks red-
den slightly.

'I'm sorry. I asked for that. I should be grateful to you,
and I am, believe me, but somehow the gratitude seems to
choke me. Makes me angrier with this impossible situation.'

Again there seemed to be an underlying suggestion of
things unsaid beneath his spoken words, but Sam was confused enough, without considering more mysteries.

'Yes, it must be frustrating,' she said, easing him to his
feet and keeping one hand on his arm until she was sure
he was balanced.

He turned and looked into her eyes. 'You don't know
the half of it, sweet Sam!'

Then he swung away, down the hall and out onto the
verandah, where she heard the tap and thump of his movement and guessed at the tenacity with which he'd practise
walking. He wasn't a man who liked being dependent on
anyone. She'd guessed that much right at the beginning.

The drive through some of Brisbane's inner suburbs did
nothing to jar his memory, and the police, while polite,
were dubious that they could be of much help. Their advice,
like everyone's, was to await the return of his memory.

'I hate feeling so beholden to you, so dependent on you
and your family.'

He put her earlier thoughts into words as they drove back
to the house.

'Don't let it worry you,' Sam assured him. 'In fact, you
won't be dependent on me, because I go back on duty tonight. I'll have a sleep this afternoon, work tonight, sleep
tomorrow. You'll be stuck with the boys for company, and
with fending for yourself when they're at uni.'

'Sean mentioned Gran. A grandmother?'

Sam saw a stationary car blocking traffic up ahead and indicated, then shifted lanes before she answered.

'Yes. My mother's mother. It's actually her house, although we all think of it as home. She's on a cruise. Back next week. If no one's claimed you by then, you'll get to meet her.'

'If no one's claimed me!' Jack grumbled. 'You're all the same, your family. Totally heartless. Talking about me like a stray animal.'

Sam shot him a smile.

'It's how we were trained,' she teased, secretly relieved he felt that way. It meant he hadn't picked up on the strange reactions she'd had earlier, when he'd fallen and she'd helped him up. Didn't realise just how far from heartless she was feeling. 'Don't get too attached to strays, our mother always said, because you know when we find the owner, you're going to have to give him back.'

'I doubt very much I have an owner,' Jack said stiffly, putting so much emphasis on the last word that Sam chuckled.

'There's that wedding ring,' she reminded him, and saw him frown, then turn away, looking out the window as if the mix of old and new along the long straight road was of utter fascination.

And this time it was he who changed the subject.

'So, back on duty tonight. In Theatre?'

Sam glanced at him.

'You don't seem to be suffering any retrograde amnesia. You're remembering things I've told you about myself. Things that have happened since the accident.'

'I am, at that,' he said calmly, still looking out the window. Then he turned towards her. '*Are* you going back to Theatre tonight? Surely there aren't operations scheduled at night, so why would the hospital have theatre nurses on duty?'

Sam scanned her emotional self and decided it was to do with the 'having to give him back to his owner' idea that made her reluctant to share too much of her life, her dreams and hopes, with him. Although, now she knew the 'there's no such thing as instant attraction' mental warning wasn't working, maybe she'd change the inner messages to 'you'll have to give him back'.

'Operating theatres? Staffed at night?'

He smiled as he prompted her with reminders of his question, and the effects of that smile fizzed along her nerves.

You'll have to give him back! She could see the words, as if printed on a cue card, in her brain.

'As a major hospital, we always have two theatres staffed at night. Smaller hospitals use on-call staff. Our theatres serve mainly as an adjunct to Accident and Emergency. A large percentage of accident victims require surgery to patch them up. Most can wait until daylight, but some can't.'

Shop-talk was good, she decided. She felt so at ease, discussing work with him.

Too at ease?

'But you still have two theatres staffed to handle emergencies?' he queried.

'Staffed, and usually in use. The transplant team often works nights, which takes one theatre. Trauma in the other.'

'And are you on duty for a specific theatre?' He sounded as if he was genuinely interested. Was that part of his charm—of the attraction she felt so strongly?

'Tonight I'll be more of a floater,' Sam told him.

'Floating hither and thither like a butterfly?'

She smiled at the image.

'You're not far wrong, only not so much hither and thither as floating between jobs.' She hesitated then decided that talking about work was safer than most subjects, so explained.

'I've recently finished a course in critical-care nursing. Since the sixties, most hospitals have been setting up intensive-care units. It started with special areas within wards for post-op patients, kind of high-dependency units, then specialised coronary-care units, the CCUs, and later Intensive Care Units, ICUs. These days most major hospitals are specialised even further, having intensive-care beds for burns patients, and separate paediatric intensive care.'

'So, having done the course, where are you headed?'

'Into the ICU, I hope. But as the new girl I'll be starting at the bottom again. In most ICUs there's a one-to-one ratio of staff to patients, but some patients, especially someone having dialytic therapy, might need two nurses in support. I'd be nurse number two.'

'Even at night the ratio is the same?'

'Night and day don't mean much in an ICU. No, I'm wrong to say that. As far as the workload is concerned, there's little difference. But people who've made a study of patients in Intensive Care have discovered it's important for rooms in an ICU to have windows, so patients are able to see the changes from day to night and back again. It's less disorientating.'

'Now disorientation is something I can relate to,' Jack said. 'Shouldn't we have turned up that street?'

'Definitely nothing wrong with your memory as far as retaining post-trauma information!' Sam said. 'We're going for a bit more of a drive, and you're supposed to be looking for familiar landmarks, not asking questions about my working life.'

'But I'm interested,' he protested, and he sounded as if he was. 'At the moment, you're floating in a room with windows. Is that it?'

Again, Sam saw the image his words provoked and she laughed.

'Oh, dear. I can just see myself flopping down on a poor defenceless patient when the fairy floating dust wore off.'

'Well?'

She glanced his way and saw him looking, not at the suburban street but at her. And something in that look, in his eyes…

She turned her attention back to the road and, hiding the jitters that intent scrutiny had caused, she continued. 'As a floater I could be called into one of the other units.'

'Coronary Care or Paediatrics?'

'Yes, but as well as that, while I'm on night duty, if they get busy in Theatre, if there's a complicated case and not enough staff to provide back-up, I could be called back there. The ICU is close to the major operating theatres so critically ill post-op patients don't have to be transported too far.'

Jack shook his head.

'It's far too complicated for me. Why the switch, anyway? Didn't you tell me you knew, from early in your training, you wanted to work in operating theatres?'

Sam nodded. This conversation was veering dangerously towards things she didn't want to discuss. Originally, she'd told herself she'd be more use in the hospital back home if she was multi-skilled, and she'd taken courses with that in mind. Even Henry had accepted her reasoning—or he had gone along with it. Until recently.

'Well?' Jack prompted, and she glanced his way and hoped her thoughts had been hidden from his keen scrutiny.

'I did want to work in Theatre, and I still enjoy it, but

there's so little patient contact involved. I mean, an all but unconscious body is wheeled in, you work on a small patch of that person, then he or she is wheeled out again.'

'And you'll have more patient contact in an ICU?' His disbelief was patent. 'I imagine most of your patients would be comatose or so drugged they're all but out to it. Not exactly chatty!'

'There's family contact. Helping their loved ones cope. And nursing challenges as well.'

It sounded weak in her own ears so heaven only knew how he'd take it.

But all he said was a polite, 'Of course.' And if he smiled as he said it, did it really matter? Why should she care what he thought?

They drove on in silence, but while it should have been uneasy, Sam found herself enjoying it. As if the air in the car had been softened in some way and now wrapped around her, offering warmth and security.

Was it a sense of companionship?

And, if so, why hadn't she felt it with Henry?

Sean was home when they returned. He helped Jack up the front steps then took him off to his study to search the internet for more information on memory loss.

'I'll fix us some lunch so you do your own thing,' he said to Sam, effectively dismissing her from any further responsibility for their guest.

Not such a bad idea, she told herself. In fact, if the niggle of emotion she felt was jealousy, it was a darned good idea. The less she saw of Jack, and the sooner he was reunited with his Jill, the better. Especially after the strange sensations she'd felt in the car. The ones that went deeper than the physical attraction.

She emptied the pack she'd been too tired to deal with the previous evening, put her dirty clothes into the washing machine and tidied everything else away. That done, she ate a solitary lunch and then, because she knew she should, she headed towards her bedroom to have a sleep.

From the raucous sounds emanating from the study, she guessed they'd abandoned the search for memory loss. She tapped on the door as she walked past.

'Not onto the X-rated sites, are you, boys?' she teased.

'Never!' Sean replied.

The door opened, and Jack stood there, leaning on his crutches so he seemed shorter, on her level, his blue eyes burning directly into hers.

'Now *that* I wouldn't allow!' he assured her. 'Though we *were* playing games.'

The twinkle in the blueness made her heart falter in its rhythm.

He's got a Jill, she reminded herself, but the reminder didn't do much good.

'Well, games won't hurt you,' she said, with as much nonchalance as she could manage under the circumstances.

'No?' he asked, his eyes intent as they scanned her face. Once again she sensed a sub-text, felt silent messages passing between them. Messages she didn't want to accept, respond to, or even acknowledge. Yet as they stood, face to face, held by some bond she didn't understand, she imagined she could feel his lips on hers, the soft rasp of his beard against her skin. Her lips parted under this imaginary kiss, and she heard his whisper.

'Sweet, sweet Sam!'

It jolted her back to reality and she blinked away the fantasy.

Surely he hadn't spoken, hadn't murmured those words.

'I—I'm off to bed,' she stuttered, hoping he wouldn't see the heat which had swept into her cheeks.

'She says that to all the men,' Sean joked. 'But don't

take it as an invitation. She's got karate moves black belts don't know about.'

'I'll have to remember that,' Jack said, but the words were directed at Sam and the huskiness in his voice gave them a very different meaning.

No way! Sam told herself as she headed for the bedroom. No way!

Instant attraction *might* actually happen. She'd concede that much. But that didn't mean she had to succumb to it. Married men were strictly off limits.

She did sleep, much to her surprise, waking late in the afternoon to find a boisterous crew gathered out the back by the pool, the boys having organised a barbecue dinner and invited friends.

Jack was reclining on one of the sun lounges, watching the activities.

'The exuberance of youth! Isn't that what it's called?' he said as Sam, drawn as irresistibly as a moth to a flame, sat down beside him.

'You're doing that "old man" thing again,' Sam warned.

He grinned at her.

'Perhaps it's the tumble I took, making me feel tired and old.' He leaned towards her, then added. 'You're quite sure about the grey hairs? None on my head? Only in the beard?'

The closeness unsettled her, but she pretended to look anyway, noticing a sheen that suggested he'd somehow managed to shampoo the over-long locks. In fact, she caught a whiff of a musky fragrance, familiar from the scented steam that often issued from the boys' bathroom.

'Only in the beard,' she said, moving back in her chair as an urge to run her fingers through that gleaming, sweet-smelling hair tickled her fingertips.

'Like the smell?' he pressed, leaning closer as she drew away. 'Pete rescued me from computer mayhem and helped me have a proper shower. Handy lads, those brothers of yours.'

'They're not bad,' Sam admitted, happier to talk about the boys than the scent of newly washed hair. 'Though liable to make a mess if I don't keep an eye on things.'

She was about to stand up when Jack's hand grabbed her arm.

'Don't go,' he said. 'They'll manage.'

Sam looked at him and saw a reflection of the confusion she was feeling in his eyes. Confusion, and something else. Something that alerted every nerve ending in her body, and started the warnings again in her head.

But they were less forceful than the messages his eyes were sending, and were further weakened by the impact of the heat his hand was generating in her skin.

'Sam?'

It was half question, half something else. A single syllable infused with so much feeling that Sam felt her toes begin to tremble, her knees go weak and her stomach clench in anticipation.

She waited, wanting, yet not wanting, to hear what he had to say. Then what had looked like ardour in his eyes turned to desperation and he cursed quietly under his breath as he turned away to stare towards the frivolity in the pool.

'No right!' she heard him mutter to himself. 'No right at all!'

And when he turned back towards her and finally spoke, it was of practical matters.

'Do you know how police systems work? If I'm listed missing in New South Wales, will it show up on a list in Queensland?'

Had she imagined what she'd seen in his eyes?

She hauled her scattered thoughts into gear, and scolded her wilful emotions for overreacting. Then went for practical herself.

'I'm sure it will. The computer systems would have to be fully integrated.' She hid the silly disappointment she was feeling behind a smile. 'After all, with no border gates, or guards, or customs, it's easy enough for a dangerous criminal to move from one state to another.'

'Good grief! I hadn't thought of that! I could be a criminal. And here I am, taking advantage of your hospitality. You shouldn't be so trusting,' he finished crossly, then he stared out across the pool again, obviously seeing things beyond the improvised game of water polo in progress in the water.

'Would I know, do you think? Know I was a cheat or a liar, a rapist or a murderer?'

'Well, it's never too late to start over,' Sam said lightly, though she knew he was seriously disturbed by the trend of his thoughts. She tried again. 'I doubt major personality changes would accompany amnesia. When I found you, you were in pain and confused. Enough to make anyone grumpy. But you were also polite, showed good manners.'

He grinned at her, and the willful emotions forgot their scolding.

'Are we eliminating murder and rape as career choices on the basis of good manners?'

She shook her head.

'On the basis of my instincts. And those of the boys. They would have accepted you as a guest and been helpful, whatever type of person you were, but they've gone further. Adopted you as a friend.'

'I should say thank you—in fact, I do thank you, and them—but shouldn't you be more wary? Less trusting? After all, a number of serial killers had wives and friends and family who had no idea what they were up to.' He stopped abruptly, frowning at her. 'Now, why would I know that?'

'Maybe you're a policeman?' Sam suggested, glad they were no longer pursuing her capacity to trust. It was hard to explain a trust that came from instinct and physiological reactions to his presence.

'From some hot climate where I wear shorts and boots?'

The teasing glint was back in his eyes and she had to remind herself that trust was one thing. But falling in love with a stranger on the strength of a pair of twinkling eyes was something else altogether!

Falling in love was definitely not on. Not with this man. Not with anyone. Not when she was more or less committed to Henry. Had been for years. Since childhood, really, if you counted their mothers' little fantasy.

And Jack was married.

You'll have to give him back!

CHAPTER SIX

Sam began her 'floating' in the ICU. It was her first hands-on experience as an ICU nurse, although she'd visited other units and had had practical sessions in several major hospitals during the training course conducted at a private hospital.

'It might seem funny, starting nights,' Wendy Barrett, the charge nurse told her, 'but it works well because the same routines are followed. However, there are fewer interruptions from visitors, or other medical staff, so you can slip more easily into our way of doing things.'

She was showing Sam around, indicating the different rooms and areas, and their functions.

'Aren't visitors here all the time? Family members?'

'Some are,' Wendy agreed. 'But where possible we try to persuade them to either go home to sleep, or at least rest in the overnight-visitors' room. It's physically as well as emotionally exhausting for those whose loved one is critically ill.'

Sam nodded, though she was unable to imagine the depths of pain one would feel at such a time.

'Do you tell the families how serious the patient's condition is?'

It was a question she and the others on the short training course had debated, and, according to the lecturer, different hospitals had different policies.

'If they ask, we try to categorise the situation. You'd have learnt about some of the scoring systems used to quantify the relationship between the severity of the condition and the eventual outcome.'

'Terrifying things like the Acute Physiology Score.' Sam nodded her agreement.

'Ha! So they taught you the APACHE! Add the Chronic Health Evaluation to the AP of the Acute Physiology and that's what you get, APACHE, but it's still subjective as far as I'm concerned. They've introduced APACHE II now, but I think experience plays a bigger part than scores. Somehow you know which patients will pull through.'

'And do you go on that gut reaction?'

Wendy smiled and shook her head.

'Not entirely. I take into account the specialist's attitude, and that of the hands-on nurses. We all seem to pull a little harder for the patients we feel are fighting for themselves, working with us. Not that we do anything differently for any patient. Perhaps it's a matter of willing them well because they're so determined themselves.'

Sam nodded.

'The fighters are the ones who survive major surgery best,' she agreed.

'Of course, that isn't what we tell families,' Wendy continued. 'We use the base knowledge we have from scoring systems like APACHE—a fit, healthy, young lad with head trauma from an accident has a better chance of survival than the eighty-year-old who was knocked down by a car outside his nursing home.' She paused, then added, 'Most of the time.'

She led Sam into a small room set up almost like a miniature operating theatre.

'But don't worry too much about it,' Wendy continued. 'You've always got the fall-back position of, ''You'll have to ask doctor about that!'' Now, this is the procedures room. Used for minor surgery, replacing a tracheostomy tube, maybe to insert deep monitoring equipment, or for dialysis, things like that. Having it here saves taking the patient to Theatre for a simple procedure. Transport of a critically ill patient is always complicated because so much gear has to go with them. And even with the gear, there's always a risk.'

They moved on.

'This is our one and only isolation room. It was built with special pressurised air-conditioning which presumably prevented bacteria-tainted air escaping into the rest of the hospital. Hence the double set of doors. Now the experts are telling us the advantage of positive-negative air pressure hasn't been proven so, no doubt, it will stop being used in future units. It has the same bedside service outlets as other rooms—two air, four suction and sixteen power. Staff must be masked, gowned and gloved at all times.'

As the room was empty, Sam could have a good look around. The services were wall-mounted and there was plenty of room around the bed for monitoring equipment. Built into one wall was a storage unit for charts, syringes, sampling tubes and suction catheters, and, by the bed, a small cabinet for patient belongings.

'As well as this special-use single room, we have four other singles. We like, whenever possible, to offer long-stay conscious patients the privacy of a single room. Three two-bed rooms make up the eleven beds on the unit.'

They made their way past the other occupied rooms, Wendy suggesting that Sam meet the patients some other time.

'Not much point when you're likely to be coming and going. You're better off familiarising yourself with our system and being a back-up on the monitors.'

She introduced Sam to the nurse on duty at the central

nurse station where monitors showed the current condition of each patient, then led her down a short passage.

'Now, these are the staff areas. There's a doctors' on-call room, though our on-call man is down in A and E or in Post-Op as often as he's here. A lot of intensivists have anaesthetic backgrounds, or physician specialty training. I guess you know that.'

'Intensivists!' Sam repeated the word. 'I wonder what it means to a layman?'

'I've never thought of that,' Wendy replied. 'I guess we do tend to speak in tongues. But, then, so do most people who have made a study of their chosen career. I'm sure a concrete-layer has conversations you and I wouldn't understand.'

An image of a bearded man in shorts and boots, pouring concrete under the hot noonday sun, flashed obligingly across Sam's mind.

She was diverted by the pager which, as a 'floater', she'd been asked to wear. It vibrated silently against her waist.

'Seems I'm wanted in Theatre,' she told Wendy, as she recognised the number she'd been asked to call.

The corridors were night-quiet, although Sam could feel the hum of activity in the air, a kind of tension that never left the hospital. Frankie Wells was the nurse in charge. She met Sam in the changing room and introduced Helen Hastings, a new anaesthetic nurse.

'I'll see you in Theatre later,' Helen said, heading for the anaesthetics room where the patient would receive a preliminary sedative.

'Emergency admission from A and E. Traffic accident,' Frankie explained to Sam. 'Must be bad as they've dragged in the new director of neurosurgery to have a look. Or maybe he was prowling the corridors, checking out his domain, when the call went out. Usually the poor resident gets stuck with night cases, and has to find whoever happens to be around to assist.'

Sam unbuttoned her uniform then grabbed a hanger to hang it up.

'Do you want a locker now you're no longer one of us and have given up your own?' Frankie asked. 'I've a spare if you want it.'

'No, thanks. I've inherited one in ICU, and left everything in that.'

Sam glanced along the row of lockers, wondering who had hers now. Thinking how quickly things changed, yet somehow stayed the same.

Frankie waited until they were both garbed in the unattractive theatre pyjamas then led the way across the clean corridor to the scrub rooms where they'd literally scrub their hands before putting on their gloves. Sam, who as circulating nurse would be in the outer, non-sterile zone of the theatre, was finished first.

'Would you get a neuro pack from the supply room?' Frankie asked. 'And a supplementary pack. Sally Cochrane is the neuro resident on duty. She's assisting the new man, so you might run into her out there. She'll have the blood typing and know what else they'll need.'

There was no sign of Sally so Sam set one of the double-wrapped packs on an instrument trolley, then slipped a smaller supplementary pack onto the bottom shelf. She inspected both for any obvious problems that could suggest contamination. Sometimes there was a tear in the paper wrapping beneath the outer plastic. Occasionally, the label, which changed colour when sterilised, showed an incomplete job had been done.

Satisfied the bundles were still sealed and had been correctly treated, she wheeled the trolley through to the theatre they'd be using.

Frankie took over, unwrapping the neuro pack to reveal a composite bundle of sterilised instruments, utensils, drapes and dressings.

'Have you met the new man?' Sam asked her. 'Do you know what instruments he favours? Should we have some split packs ready, or extra instruments in case he wants something special?'

'That'll be your job,' Frankie replied. 'You'll be the go-fer. As far as I know, no one on the nursing staff has run into the man. This time of year, with most of the theatres still closed down for cleaning, and staff on leave, you don't expect to have to deal with the big boss.'

Sam nodded. 'Not that it makes a difference who we deal with,' she said. 'I reckon adaptability has to be a prime requisite for a good theatre nurse.'

'Which is why you should have stuck with it,' Frankie told her. 'I still can't understand this sudden urge of yours to change to Intensive Care. And as for taking a course in January, when most people are partying...'

'It was only a short course,' Sam protested. 'A summer-school thing! I wanted to see if I liked it. I've been thinking of doing a Master's, and ICU seemed like a good choice.'

She didn't add that it was something she could study externally. Something to keep her connected to her nursing, if she stopped work to have the family Henry wanted.

That's if she finally decided to say yes to Henry.

She sighed at the thought but fortunately, at that moment, the patient was wheeled in. Her mind focussed on her work and she watched as the anaesthetist, Harry Strutt, slid an endotracheal tube into the sleeping patient and taped it into place. Sally Cochrane appeared, her eyes smiling at Sam from behind protective glasses.

'We'll need a laminectomy frame,' she said, and Sam

followed her out to the store for the awkward steel and styrofoam frame that held a patient prone on the table.

With Frankie's help, Sam set it in place on the operating table, while Sally catheterised the man.

'Now all we have to do is get him over onto the table,' Sally muttered, looking at the patient, who was far from slim.

'We'll manage it if we move together,' Harry suggested. 'Helen, you watch the screens while I lend a hand. Who's doing this with you, Sally? Another resident? An intern? Where is he—or she?'

'Getting his orders from God, I presume,' Sally muttered, and Sam, who'd often worked with Sally in Theatre, turned to glance at the surgeon.

'Figure of speech,' Sally murmured. 'New bosses always make me edgy. Are we ready to lift?'

Together, they managed to roll the man over onto the frame, and a soft sighing of the door suggested their timing was spot on. The new boss had arrived.

Sam stood back out of the way as the man strode towards the table, a slighter, less authoritative figure, trotting at his heels.

The surgeon was tall, solid-looking and as anonymous as the rest of the theatre staff in his green paper pyjamas, slippers, cap and mask. Although, unlike the rest of the operating team who had on their special protective eye wear, this man wore glasses. Presumably to correct a defect.

'My name's Grant Hudson. I'm the new director of Neurosurgery.' His voice was deep, and somehow familiar, but that could have been because all voices were slightly muffled by the masks so they sounded much the same.

'This patient was involved in a single-vehicle accident,' he continued. 'Rolled his car, and presented with some numbness in his feet. It's ascending, travelling up his body.

By the time he was given his preliminary sedation he'd lost feeling in his hands.'

He glanced around and his eyes seemed to find and focus on Sally.

'I believe he's got an epidural clot somewhere along the spinal cord. They're rare, but it's all that could explain a progressive loss of feeling in his limbs. The deterioration suggests it's getting bigger, following the line of his spine, and causing more and more problems. I would normally do a myelogram to see if we could locate the exact site of the problem, but the paralysis is progressing so rapidly it could cause permanent damage if we wait the couple of hours we'd need for injecting the dye and then taking the scan.'

'So he's going to cut open the man's spine to find it,' Sally murmured.

'No, Dr Cochrane,' the specialist's deep voice contradicted. 'You're the one who needs the practice. *You're* going to cut open the man's spine to find it.'

Sam shivered. There was an implacability in the man's voice that unsettled her, made her glad she was only a bit-part player in this little drama. And an arrogance about the man's announcement that puzzled her.

She was used to surgeons explaining their procedures for the benefit of students who might be in attendance, but at this time of the year, with no audience? Perhaps he was explaining for the benefit of Sally and the intern.

Sam puzzled over it as she watched. Frankie handed Sally the knife for the first cut, and the new man indicated the length of cut he wanted, about eighteen inches from the nape of the patient's neck, down almost to his waist.

A very long exploratory incision! Did he worry that he'd guessed incorrectly? That he wasn't opening up the man for nothing?

Once that first incision was made, Sally used an electrocautery pen to peel the muscle back from the spinal bones. Grant Hudson helped, working with her, lifting out debris, keeping the site clean, checking on Frankie as she loaded instruments and padding and passed them on to Sally. It was painstaking work, but soon the long ridge of laminated bones was revealed.

'Muscle grows back,' the new man said, still explaining, talking them all through the operation.

'It will soon heal,' he said, as if he, too, might be intimidated by the size of the hole Sally had created. 'Now the laminate. Punch through that.'

Frankie passed the long-handled punch to Sally and Sam thought she saw the younger doctor's fingers shake as she took it. But her hands were steady as she used the tool to bite off tiny pieces of the lamina shingles which protect the spinal cord, searching for the clot they were assuming was there. And for what seemed like a long time, the ting of the bone fragments dropping into a metal dish held by the resident were the only noises in the room.

As time passed, Frankie mopped Sally's brow, then indicated to Sam to bring in drinks which she held to the doctors' lips, carefully manoeuvring straws up under their masks.

The new chief shook his head when she held a drink towards him. A mobile phone sent its muted melody sounding through the silence, and Helen, who'd picked it up from the bottom of the anaesthetist's trolley where surgeons invariably stowed their phones and pagers, held it towards the man. He indicated she should answer it, then hold it near his ear. He listened, then spoke quietly for several minutes, before stepping away and letting Helen press the end button.

Sam wondered if this interruption would break what was an uncommon silence in the theatre, but no one came up with a joke, about mobiles or anything else, and Sally continued chipping at the lamina. Crunch, then ting, crunch then ting—tension that couldn't be conducive to good surgery, building higher and higher.

'Grab another Kerrison punch for me, please, Sam, and more dressings,' Frankie asked, when the excavation had been going on for more than ninety minutes. 'The punch will be getting slippery with all the blood and I need more packing.'

Sam slipped away, relieved to get out of the room, found the instrument and a bundle of packing, checked both were sealed and properly sterilised and returned. She held the bundle in one hand, and the punch in the other, intending to whip the protective bag off it and slip it to Frankie to hand to Sally as soon as she indicated she was ready, but it was the new surgeon who turned to take it.

As Sam saw his face for the first time—or what there was to see of it, above the mask and beneath the cap—she was struck by the blue eyes behind prescription glasses. Familiar blue eyes, framed by the mask and cap in the same way dark hair and a beard framed another pair.

Her body went numb. So numb her fingers relaxed their grip and she dropped the punch on the floor, the clang of metal, even through the paper wrapping, startling everyone.

'Get a clean one in case the paper tore,' the surgeon snapped, and Sam thrust the packing at Frankie and hurried out again. As she left the room she heard a rumble of his voice, probably telling Frankie what he thought of incompetent nurses.

But Sam was beyond caring what the man had said. One sentence was hammering in her head. Five simple words which had seemed so comical when she'd heard them uttered.

My brother's a brain surgeon!

Now they echoed in her mind, while she told herself, firmly, that many men had blue eyes and the similarity was pure coincidence.

And what were the odds, even if Jack did have a brain surgeon brother, that she'd end up working with him?

A couple of thousand to one?

Impossible!

But *her* hands were shaking now, her inner turmoil showing in this physical manifestation.

What was she supposed to do? Ask the man if he'd lost a brother?

Don't be stupid!

She grabbed another instrument and hurried back, handing it to Frankie, then retreating to the shadows again.

But she couldn't escape his voice, which earlier had seemed vaguely familiar and now seemed even more so.

They found the beginning of the clot, as red and rawlooking as fresh meat, near the third thoracic vertebrae.

'Follow it up,' Grant Hudson ordered, without any apparent relief that his guess had proved correct. 'It's been oozing slowly, causing increasing pressure down the length of the cord, which explains the progressive nature of his paralysis.'

The operation proceeded, the bleeding veins cauterised, the area examined for any further damage, then the wound closing began.

'I'll leave you to it,' the specialist told Sally. 'You have my pager number if you need me.'

Sam watched him depart with a mix of relief and frustration. He'd be leaving the hospital, and probably not returning until well after she'd gone off duty. And even if this patient went to the ICU, department directors usually did their ward rounds during the day, preferring to sleep through the night shift when Sam would be on duty.

Not that nurses could 'drop in' on medical directors any-way. Not without running the gauntlet of the department secretary.

She tried to remember if she knew the neuro secretary. Easier to explain a possible lost brother to someone she knew and liked than to one of the unknown dragon-ladies who guarded the top men at the hospital.

'You still working here?' Frankie asked, and Sam turned her attention back to the operation.

'More tape.' Frankie's voice suggested it was the second time she'd asked, and as the scrub nurse repeated the code for the required dressing, Sam hurried off.

Perhaps Grant Hudson was still in the tearoom.

She couldn't check now.

She found the tape and returned to Theatre, in time to catch the end of Sally's complaint about the new man.

'I can handle anyone as long as they have a sense of humour but, honestly, there he was, standing in theatre garb that was obviously four sizes too small and yelling at me for laughing.'

'Sounds like a long few years ahead of you, Sal,' the anaesthetist said.

'Not years, year. I finish this December, and then I'm out of here. Someone else can put up with him.'

'But first you have to survive the year,' Frankie reminded her.

'Well, he'll have to survive it as well. If he thinks I'm going to kowtow to him, he's got another think coming.'

Laughter greeted this brave stance, but Sam didn't join in. The man had intimidated her enough to wonder if Sally might be making a mistake in taking him on.

Or was it simply because she was concerned about Jack that the man had sent shivers up her spine?

It was close to dawn by the time they'd finished in

Theatre, then, knowing the patient would be sent from Recovery to the ICU, for a few days at least, she said no to a cup of tea and headed back to the specialised ward to help prepare a bed for him.

Wendy greeted her with relief.

'Talk about all hell breaking out the moment we lose a staff member. We've had a cardiac arrest. The nurse called a code then realised it was one of our NFR patients. By that time, of course, the troops had arrived and we had to send everyone away again and await the inevitable.'

'How do you know who doesn't want resuscitation?' Sam asked as her mind translated the initials into Not For Resuscitation. 'I assume it's on the charts?'

'It should be on a huge placard hung above the bed, or around a patient's neck in case he arrests on his way somewhere, but it looks a bit cold and heartless. Yes, it's on the chart, in large capital letters, but who looks at charts when a patient's heart stops beating?'

'Who tells the family?' Sam asked. 'Do you get a doctor in?'

'We have to have a doctor anyway, so he or she usually does it. If there's a family member present, there's no need to actually tell. All we can do is offer comfort and support.'

Sam nodded, thinking of the room she'd seen earlier—the crying room, as it was called. Most ICUs had one of these, off the visitors' lounge. A place where people could be alone while they dealt with their emotional reactions to either good or bad news.

They were setting up a room for the neuro patient as they chatted, an orderly bringing in the Stryker frame. Once set up on a bed, it could be used to turn paraplegic patients so they escaped the worst of pressure sores and thrombophlebitis, the forming of painful and potentially deadly clots in the veins.

'Used one of these before?'

Sam nodded.

'During a stint in Orthopaedics. As far as I can remember, that pin at the head of the frame prevents accidental rotation and the main rule was to always put the arm boards and table away before rotating.'

'That's enough to begin with,' Wendy told her. 'Up here, we've a policy of always having two nurses present for rotation. That way, one checks on what the other does. Whoever is working with you will give the instructions, so just follow what she tells you.'

She went on to give Sam a refresher course in Stryker characteristics, pointing out how the lower part of the frame could be removed, the arm boards adjusted to raise or lower the upper end of the frame, and the locking device that clicked into place when the frame was horizontal.

'There's a chart in the locker which explains maximum elevation for different conditions but the doctors will write in what they want in the way of movement.'

As she talked, Sam realised that this would be 'her' patient. Her responsibility tomorrow night and for the succeeding nights, as long as he remained in the ICU.

Responsibility!

The word brought Jack to mind. Not that he'd been absent from it for long.

Wendy glanced at her watch.

'If we haven't heard he's on his way by now, it means he won't be here until we're off duty. Do you want a cuppa?'

Suddenly, a cuppa sounded most appealing. Sam realised how hungry she was.

'Do you know the new neurosurgeon?' she asked Wendy, as they joined another ICU nurse in the tearoom.

'Grant Hudson?' Wendy shook her head. 'I saw a blurb

about his arrival in the latest hospital newsletter. Great-looking bloke, if his photo hasn't been touched up. Don't tell me he was up in Theatre with you?'

'And how!' Sam told her. 'I don't think I've ever heard a quieter operation. Harry Strutt was doing the anaesthetic and he's never chatty, but Sally Cochrane has a tribe of brothers and has always had an unending supply of rude jokes. She usually keeps everyone laughing.'

'But not last night?' Wendy said, and Sam shook her head.

'Total silence! You could have cut the atmosphere with a knife.'

'Or scalpel,' Wendy joked.

'Maybe they'd had an argument in the changing room,' Ann, the other nurse, suggested.

'But Sally would have changed in ours,' Sam explained. 'There's always been strict segregation of the sexes in theatre changing rooms.'

Ann and Wendy both chuckled.

'You've been away longer than you realise,' Wendy told her. 'The changing-room revolution was also explained in the New Year newsletter. Apparently, some of the doctors feel they'll gain more, changing with other doctors rather than nurses and orderlies. Mixed changing rooms now prevail. If you changed in your usual room, then the room previously used by the men is now the doctors' room and you'll have Bill Trotter, and whatever other male theatre nurses there are, changing in with the women.'

'Élitism, that's what it is!' Ann muttered, but Sam admitted she could see some point in it.

'Although,' she argued, 'the crosspollination of doctors and nurses using the same changing rooms has always helped in building a team spirit in Theatre. That mightn't work as well now.'

'Certainly didn't last night,' Wendy commented, 'if your observations are correct.'

But Sam had a feeling that the lack of empathy within the team stemmed from the team leader's attitude rather than the switch in changing rooms.

Poor Jack, if the man *did* turn out to be his brother!

CHAPTER SEVEN

SEAN was waiting on the front verandah as Sam pulled into the drive.

'Your visitor's sick as a dog.' Her brother came galloping down the stairs to give her the bad news. 'We've been up all night with him. Finally called an after-hours medical service and got a chap who looked younger than Pete and I. He said Jack had a fever.'

Sean shook his head in disgust as he relayed this information.

'As if we hadn't already figured that out.'

'A fever and what else?' Sam asked, anxiety knotting inside her chest.

'Bad headache. Pains in his joints. Says his eyes hurt but that could be the headache.'

Sam closed her eyes. Not only had she brought a stranger into their home, but now it seemed possible she'd exposed the twins to unknown health risks. Unless the fever was caused by a cerebral haemorrhage of some kind.

'Pete thought the cut on his chin might have become infected, but we shaved around it and there's no sign of redness or pus.'

'What do you mean, you shaved around it? Just the cut, or did you take off all his beard?'

'Just around the cut,' Sean explained, following her as she took the stairs two at a time. 'Guy's too sick to be wanting someone shaving him.'

She should have been prepared, but when she saw her 'stray' immobile on the bed, his face flushed, the tattered remnants of his once luxurious beard clinging like seaweed to his chin, her heart ached for him, and she had to blink back tears.

She walked quietly into the room and knelt by the bed, her hand reaching out automatically to feel his forehead.

Jack's eyes opened and she saw confusion change to relief. Then he clasped her hand and held it tightly, and he muttered the words she'd once imagined him saying. 'Sweet, sweet Sam.'

He's delirious, she reminded herself. And rather than going into raptures, think practical. If he's even partially awake, you should be getting some fluids into him.

She slid one arm behind his back and eased his shoulders off the pillow. She saw his eyes open again, and what seemed like an echo of the words appear in them.

'Can't have you love a stranger. Stupid. Dangerous.' His voice was raspy but the meaning came through loud and clear, then he sipped at the water she offered until his body became heavier and she knew he'd drifted back to sleep.

And he's right, Sam told herself. Especially a married stranger.

But could you turn off love? She realised she had no experience of the type of emotion she was feeling for Jack—so she didn't know the answer.

Although she suspected it was impossible.

Like turning off the tides.

She stayed for a while, smoothing damp tendrils of hair back from his face, thinking of what might have been.

And of Henry who had never generated anything beyond a mild curiosity with his kisses.

Could she marry Henry, knowing she had the ability to feel so much more for someone?

Even if the someone wasn't available?

Wouldn't marrying Henry under such circumstances be

offering him second best? Cheating him of the opportunity to feel this way himself?

She sighed and frowned down at the sleeping man who had prompted all these unanswerable questions. Then she smiled as she realised that, whatever happened, it was worth it to know she could feel the way he made her feel.

That she could be as one with another human being.

A muted groan from the bed reminded her of her responsibilities and she banished the fanciful thoughts and went in search of her brothers.

'Did the doctor leave any tablets? A prescription?'

Pete shook his head.

'He said to give him aspirin, but he took blood and sputum. Said he'd send both to the labs for testing. He asked who was Jack's regular GP so we told him Dr Charlton. The test results will go to him.'

'Cost us a fortune, too,' Sean put in. 'Guy's got no name, no medicare card. We had to pay full fee, up front, before the doctor would even look at him.'

Sam hoped they were joking. She'd heard stories about after-hours services but paying up front seemed unbelievable.

However, right now she had other concerns.

'Did the doctor suggest more tests? Did you tell him about the head injury? That the fever could be a result of his fall?'

His fall!

Cracked skulls and infection!

Meningitis and encephalitis were now looming large in her panicked brain, while her heart began a panicky jitter at the thought of Jack being so seriously ill.

'We told him all of that,' Pete replied. 'How else could we explain a fellow who'd lost his memory?'

'He had X-rays!' Sam muttered, and she all but ran from the room, back to where they'd put their visitor.

The blue envelope was on top of a chest of drawers.

Sam checked that Jack was still asleep, seized the envelope and hurried out again.

Yes! They had X-rayed his head. From various angles. She held the films up to the light, searching the whitish bone for a darker line that might indicate a hairline fracture.

There was nothing she could see, but her fear for this man she had to give back wasn't so easily allayed.

'If you two have been up all night, you should go to bed now,' she told her brothers, hoping a practical approach might offset the fear.

'No way! We're off to uni. You're the one who'll need to sleep. In fact, you'd better take the second bed in Jack's room. Sleep in there. That way you'll wake if he needs you.'

She agreed to this plan, but didn't tell them that wild horses wouldn't keep her far away from him.

Her own plan, to mention the name Grant Hudson to Jack, was shot to pieces. The man couldn't remember much when he was well. What hope would he have when he was in the grip of febrile confusion?

She made herself a cup of coffee then checked the refrigerator and pantry shelves. He'd need plenty of fluids. Fortunately, with the twins in the house, fruit juice was high on the shopping list each week and she'd stocked up on it before she'd gone bush.

A loud cry sent her flying back towards his bedroom.

Empty.

She found him in the bathroom, clad in a pair of borrowed boxer shorts, uneasily balanced between one crutch and the washbasin as he stared with disbelief at his reflection.

'Look at me!' he stormed as she came racing in. 'Look at my face! Did you do this?'

The blue eyes darted angry fire.

'The twins wanted to check your stitches,' she said, moving forward to steady him and feeling the burn of fever in his skin. 'They thought an infection might explain your illness.'

'I can't stay looking like this,' he told her, the anger not a jot abated by her explanation. 'I need a razor.'

'And how do you think you're going to manage shaving?' she demanded, anxiety for him fuelling her own rage. 'You're shaking like a leaf, and can't stand up without support. How are you going to hold a razor even if I did give you one? In your toes?'

The glowering look he shot at her, via the mirror, should have been enough, but he had more spleen to vent.

'Fine nurse you turned out to be!' He used scorn to emphasise the words. 'What happened to kindness and compassion? To the gentle touch?'

Sam, tired, worried and totally confused by whatever it was that was going on inside her body in spite of all her mental warnings, returned his glower with a glare of her own.

'The gentle touch is going to be a kick on your sore ankle if you don't get yourself back to bed right now!' she told him. 'And if you need to use the bathroom again, please, call me first. At least that way I can give you a hand. The twins are gone and you're far too big for me to pick up off the floor if you keel over.'

'So leave me there!' he snorted, and Sam, belatedly realising how ridiculous the argument had become, gave a gurgle of laughter.

'And trip over you every time I walk down the hall? I don't think so.'

She moved her hand so she could grip his biceps and give him some support.

'Come on. Back to bed for you. If you like, I'll shave the rest of your face. I had to learn about shaving in one of my early prac. sessions. Although it wasn't always faces we shaved.'

Jack shot her a look of undisguised horror.

'Ouch!' he muttered. 'Thanks but, no, thanks. I'd rather wait until your brothers come home.'

Then, as they began to move, he groaned.

'Foot or head hurting?' Sam asked.

'All over hurting,' he replied. 'Every bone. And especially my back. Do you think I might have broken something else when I fell?'

His voice was weak and breathy, indicative of pain taking its toll.

'Perhaps a rib or two,' Sam offered, although she knew it wasn't likely. He'd have felt the pain as they'd walked out of the rainforest. This was something new.

She helped him back to bed, drew a sheet up over him and watched, with some concern, as sleep claimed him almost immediately.

The kettle had just boiled for the cup of coffee she needed to help her think when the phone rang.

'Where's this relation of yours been that he might have picked up dengue fever?'

Sam recognised Dr Charlton's voice. He'd been their holiday GP since they were children. And his abrupt way of demanding information hadn't changed over the years.

'He's not exactly a relative,' Sam managed to explain, while her mind struggled to assimilate dengue fever. 'Is it catching? Quarantinable? The twins had friends over last night. And Jack had his leg set at Beaudesert hospital. The man's been in contact with dozens of people in the last few days. And I've been with him, then in Theatre and the ICU.'

Her voice rose as panic over the consequences escalated.

'Jack Abbot? And he's not a relative?'

Trust Dr C. to lock on to the one thing she didn't consider important at this stage.

Restraining an urge to scream at him, she managed to say calmly enough, 'I can't explain it all now, but you're sure that's what it is?'

'His white blood cell count is way down, showing a viral infection of some kind. Apparently the lab technician who caught the job had nothing much to do during the night, so he took it a bit further and tested for the off-beat. Mind you, no local lab would see much of dengue. Could be the tech simply looked at a picture in a book and decided it was close enough.'

'But is it catching?' Sam demanded, cutting into Dr Charlton's opinion of the lab tech's ability.

'Only if you have a special supply of *Aëdes* mosquitoes in the house and one bites your patient and then bites you. They're tropical mosquitoes, Sam. You should be safe.'

'And the house is screened,' she said thankfully, although the doctor seemed convinced the *Aëdes* wouldn't be living in Toowong.

'So what do I do with him?' she asked the doctor.

'Give him aspirin and plenty of fluids. It's a two-stage affair. He might get completely better for a day or two then get worse. A rash usually appears with the second rise in temperature. Looks a lot like scarlet fever, from what I've read. I've never had a patient with it. I might drop in.'

A buzzing in her ear told her the doctor considered the conversation finished.

'Great! Now he's going to be a showcase for dengue fever!' Sam muttered as she hung up. But she forgot her coffee, hurrying to the study where she kept her medical books, anxious to look up their guest's infection now it had a name.

Half an hour later she knew a little more about dengue fever. Enough to know there wasn't any treatment and all she could do was see that Jack was cared for through his illness.

Back in the kitchen she filled an insulated jug with juice and ice and set it on a tray with a clean glass, a bowl of water and a soft handtowel she could moisten and wipe across his body to reduce his temperature.

She added a bottle of aspirin which was getting close to its use-by date, so rarely did any of them have a use for analgesics, then carried the tray through to his bedroom.

He was tossing restlessly, and she bathed him first, then offered him a drink.

He opened his eyes and blinked as if surprised to see her, then recognition and understanding must have dawned for he sat up, winced, then said fretfully, 'I can't stay here! Shouldn't have come in the first place. I'm making work for you. Nothing but trouble. And you're working nights, woman! You should be sleeping, not offering drinks to useless invalids.'

'Finished your little spiel?' Sam teased. 'Did talking make you thirsty? Here.'

She handed him the glass of juice, the sides already frosted by condensation.

'Drink!' she ordered. 'You've got dengue fever so maybe you *have* been in Sumatra.'

'Damn mosquitoes. I used a net. I rubbed on repellent. *And* stayed indoors at night. Wretched things used to seek me out. Dengue, eh? Well, that's a change.'

He was sipping at the drink as he spoke, his face and voice reflective.

'Change from what?' Sam asked gently, anxious to pursue this indication of memory, yet not wanting to upset him again.

He turned towards her and as she looked into his eyes she felt that link again, that physical ripple effect which touch had first provoked. He belongs to Jill, or Jocelyn, she reminded herself, eyeing his wedding ring in the hope that a visual confirmation might send a stronger message to her body.

You'll have to give him back.

The look turned into a frown, accompanied by a helpless lifting of the shoulders in a despairing shrug.

'I don't know,' he admitted. 'For a moment there I thought I had something.'

Sam broke the tension with a laugh.

'If you were living in the tropics you probably did!' she told him. 'There's always a choice of somethings to be had in hot climates. Malaria, typhoid, any number of horrible infestations.'

'Which is another reason I shouldn't be staying here.' He spoke gruffly and tried to move, but Sam's hand on his shoulder, exerting minimum pressure, was enough to prevent him rising.

'Relax!' she told him. 'We won't catch anything. I've checked it out. What's more, our local GP, who also happens to be courting our grandmother, is so intrigued by the diagnosis he's going to visit you. Although, from the way he spoke, he'd prefer to see the rash so he might wait a day or two. If I let you go, he'll never forgive me and I'll have a dreadful relationship with my step-grandfather, if Gran ever decides to say yes.'

Jack closed his eyes and shook his head, then opened them again to ask, 'Are you normal? Is your family considered average? Is this how ordinary people go on in real life? Pete and Sean are like a stand-up comedy routine, and you want me to stay here for fear of upsetting a possible step-grandfather.'

'We're normal for us!' Sam said, her hackles rising at the implied criticism of her family.

Her defensive tone must have alerted him, for he reached out and touched her lightly on the arm.

'Of course you are. Don't ever change. I think this fever might be making me a bit grouchy.'

Sam had been jolted by the touch, but she rallied.

'Fever, broken ankle, concussion and amnesia. I guess that's enough to excuse a modicum of grouchiness.' She saw him smile and felt her own lips widen in response. 'Just don't overdo it.

'And forget about leaving here,' she added, when the smiling at each other thing seemed to have gone on for too long. And the silent messages were once again making her think things she shouldn't think. 'We might be mad, we Abbots, but once we take on a job we see it through. You're stuck with us until someone claims you, or you remember who you are.'

Now was the time to mention Grant Hudson, she realised, but the fingers which had remained resting on her arm suddenly slid off, and when she looked at her patient she saw his eyes had closed. Sleep had claimed him again.

But it hadn't wiped away his smile.

She left him, had a shower and pulled on a light, loose shift dress with a swirling pattern of different coloured greens. She'd be comfortable in it if she did happen to fall asleep, and look far more decent than she had in the Garfield T-shirt.

But she'd barely settled on the second bed in the spare room than an image of the specialist's eyes flashed through her head.

Grant Hudson.

Perhaps she could phone him. Ask if he had a brother. It was after nine. If he was anything like the other doctors she knew, he'd be at work—in spite of his sleepless night.

Heading back into the kitchen, she phoned the hospital switchboard and asked to be put through.

Experience told her to expect a secretary, and so she wasn't surprised when a woman's voice announced she'd reached Dr Hudson's office and enquired as to her business.

Sam gave her name, explained she was a nurse at the hospital, then asked to speak to the doctor.

'On what matter?' the dragon guarding his inner sanctum demanded.

'It's personal,' Sam told her, not wanting to get too deeply into someone else's business with a stranger.

'He doesn't take personal calls during working hours,' the dragon told her, spitting out each word so carefully that Sam imagined she could feel an accompanying brush of fire.

'Not even from his brother?' Sam tried in desperation.

'You are obviously not his brother!' the woman told her, and once again a buzzing in her ear told Sam she'd been disconnected.

'Buzzing in my ears. Ripples in my skin. Maybe *I've* got something contagious,' she grumbled to herself.

But she refused to admit defeat. She sat and thought for a while, then had a brainwave.

She'd try again.

No good. The dragon would hang up.

Disguise her voice. Now, how on earth did one do that?

Handkerchief over the phone. She'd seen that in a movie. But perhaps she'd just sound sinister.

Mobile phone. They always distorted voices.

She retrieved her mobile from her handbag and dialled again, getting through to the switchboard first.

She gave her name and, using the feeble excuse of forgetfulness, asked for the name of Dr Hudson's secretary. Then asked to be put through to the dragon.

'Oh, Miss Flintock,' Sam said, using her most cultured tones. 'It's Jocelyn here. Could I speak to Grant, please?'

There was a rustling of papers and Sam thought she heard the name Jocelyn muttered under the dragon's breath. 'He's not here at the moment, Miss Milson,' Miss Flintock told her. 'But I'll tell him you phoned and ask him to return your call. Is there any particular time that would suit you?'

So much for not taking personal calls in work hours, Sam thought to herself, but she maintained the deception, making up an excuse of uncontactability and inquiring when Grant might be in the office.

'It's hard to say,' Miss Flintock told her. 'He should take a lunchbreak at one but, perhaps because he's new and wants to find his way around, he rarely comes back here during the day. I use the phone and pager to contact him with messages.'

'Well, could you tell him I phoned?' Sam admitted defeat, although Miss Flintock's words had given her another idea. If she phoned after hours, when the dragon was off duty, maybe he'd pick up his own phone.

'Oh, wait a minute, he's just come in.' The disembodied voice became fainter as she spoke to her boss. 'Miss Milson for you, Doctor. If you go through to your office, I'll put it through.'

Sam waited, not wanting to hope.

So he knew someone called Jocelyn! That still wasn't proof.

And now she had to explain.

There were a series of clicks then the remembered voice,

not at all distorted by the mobile, demanded, 'Jocelyn, have you heard from him?'

'I'm not Jocelyn,' Sam began, her heart quaking as she realised this wasn't going to be as easy as she'd imagined. 'I'm the nurse who dropped the punch in Theatre last night.'

She heard an explosion of disbelief at the other end of the phone and rushed on.

'But if she's a friend of your brother's—if you have a brother, that is. If that's who you were asking if she'd heard from—'

Sam stumbled out the thwarted sentences, then realised she might as well save her breath. Once again a familiar buzzing in her ear told her that someone didn't want to chat with her.

And the dragon lady wouldn't fall for the Jocelyn routine again.

Which left Sam with the option of tracking him down at the hospital. Coming face to face with him somewhere and asking him.

But first she needed to sleep. She returned to the spare bedroom. Her patient was sleeping, but flushed and restless. The fever was far from abating. If anything, it seemed to be worsening—although the twins had had a grim night, so it might be peaking again.

Sam sponged his forehead, then ran the damp cloth down his arms, held it against his wrist, then bathed his face again, his neck, across the top of his torso.

He muttered unintelligibly, opened his eyes and looked at her, took her hand and held it in his. He gave a soft sigh that might have been contentment—or perhaps relief—then he closed his eyes again.

'It might be the public's perception of a nurse's duty,

but I can't sit and hold your hand all day,' Sam whispered to him when she was sure he was sleeping soundly.

She eased her fingers out of his now relaxed clasp but didn't move away immediately, studying him instead. Smiling to herself as she questioned what she could possibly find attractive in a half shaven, half hairy individual who'd plummeted into her life like a misfired rocket.

And almost certainly belonged to someone else.

'You'll have to be given back, you know,' she said softly, and felt a stab of sheer regret in the region of her heart.

Don't be stupid, she added to herself, and on that admonishment she moved, crossing the space between the two beds and settling on the spare.

'Something's ringing. Where's your phone?'

Sam groaned and shifted her position as a small, hard object jabbed her in the ribs. Remembering where she was and why, she shot into a sitting position. The invalid she was supposed to be caring for was leaning over between the two beds and poking her with the tip of one crutch.

'I'd have gone looking for it but you expressly forbade me to get out of bed on my own in case I fell over and caused an obstruction in the passage.'

Sam blinked as she tried to assimilate the information, then blinked again.

'You're feeling better?'

He smiled at her, causing so much heat to shimmer down her spine that she wondered if she might have caught his fever.

'Not only that,' he began, nodding to answer her question, 'but...'

The ringing noise began again and Sam, realising it was

the front doorbell not the phone, lifted herself off the bed and hurried down the hall.

She opened the door and blinked yet again as the well-built, respectably suited young man filled her vision.

'Henry!'

'Well, don't sound so surprised to see me,' he said jovially, coming in and greeting her with a bear hug. 'Today's the day I told you I'd be down.'

He bent his head to kiss her and Sam twisted slightly so his lips pressed against her cheek.

'Today's the day,' he repeated in a Henry kind of whisper that seemed to echo through the house.

Sam opened her mouth to say something—anything—but no words would come. Fortunately, Henry didn't seem to notice. He bent over to pick up his overnight bag, talking all the time, relaying messages from her family, the recent rainfall data, how well the country was looking and how the change in the weather patterns from El Niño to La Niña would be good for everyone.

'Dump my bag in the spare room as usual?'

Finally something penetrated Sam's fog of confusion.

'No. Not the spare room!' she spluttered. 'You can put your bag in my bedroom.'

Henry looked stunned.

No, stunned was too mild a description. Poleaxed.

'I don't know, Sam,' he said, hesitation slowing down the flow of words. 'Your parents... We've never talked about that kind of thing... By saying today's the day, I didn't mean—'

Sam's already bewildered brain found it all too much.

'What kind of thing?' she demanded. 'And what do my parents have to do with where you sleep? What are you babbling about, Henry?'

Then, as Henry's usually pale skin took on a rosy hue, she caught on.

'Oh Henry! Today is definitely not the day for that! I'll sleep in Gran's room. I've got someone else in the spare room. He's contagious.'

The contagion idea came to her in a flash of sheer brilliance. One certain way to keep Henry and Jack apart.

'But you came out of the spare room,' he protested. 'I saw your movement through the glass. And you knew I was coming. I always use the spare room.'

Sam felt a great wave of tiredness wash over her. She grabbed his bag out of his hand and led the way to her bedroom.

'There!' she said, dropping it on the floor. 'The sheets are almost clean. I had a sleep on it yesterday afternoon, but I've been on night duty since then and nursing our other house guest.'

Seeing Henry's face and realising that his confusion was almost equalling her own, she added more kindly, 'I'll explain it all later, but right now you must be tired after the trip. Would you like a shower—or perhaps a swim to freshen up? From the noises downstairs I'd say one or other of the boys has just come home. That's the end of peace and quiet. Come through to the kitchen when you're ready and I'll make you a cup of tea.'

She walked away, pretending not to notice the movement he'd made towards her. Which was silly as they'd been 'kissing cousins' for many years and there'd been times when she'd quite enjoyed Henry's kisses.

As she left the room she saw Pete disappear into the spare bedroom.

Good! He could check on their invalid and she'd make tea for Henry. Keep the pair of them apart.

Which worked for an hour, while Henry drank his tea,

told Sam, in intricate detail, how his accountancy business was progressing, and then regaled her with the trials and tribulations of the local council who were apparently refusing to rezone some land he'd bought for development.

'I mean, it's right on the edge of town. You know the parcel. Ideal for light industrial development—small factories, a storage facility.'

'But it's in the green belt the council want to keep around the town,' Sam reminded him. 'It always has been.'

'Yes, but that's a short-term view of things. I've spoken to several councillors who agree with me. I know I'll sway the rest. In time.'

By wearing them down, Sam thought, then realised it was what Henry had been doing to her for as long as she could remember. Wearing her down. Telling her what a perfect match they'd make. Agreeing with her plans to continue studying but always seeing them in his terms. Her additional training would be a benefit to the local hospital when she eventually returned there to work.

'I'd better check on my patient. I won't be long.'

She excused herself and headed for the spare bedroom, although she knew her presence there wasn't necessary. Pete was with their guest, and more than capable of tending to the man.

He was sitting on the bed, not tending at all. In fact, it looked more as if they were chatting.

Chatting? When Jack had been so feverish only a few hours earlier?

'Henry's here, then? Blocking the drive with that gasguzzler of his. As usual!' Pete directed his complaint at Sam then turned to Jack. 'Henry is our so-dear cousin twice or thrice removed. His mum and our mum are cousins so you can figure out the remove. He's been courting Sam in a desultory fashion for about a hundred years.'

'Long courtship,' Jack murmured, his blue eyes snagging Sam's attention although she'd tried to avoid them. 'Can't bring him up to scratch? Can't get him to pop the question? Is that the problem, Sam?'

She stared at him in disbelief.

'You must be feeling better to be giving cheek.' Then she realised what he'd said and frowned. 'Well, just remember, you're a temporary resident in this house, and any trouble from you and busking might become your only option.'

'Busking?' Pete echoed.

'At the hospital. I suggested it,' Jack said, and Sam's frown deepened. She knew a fever could break as suddenly as it flared, but usually a patient was tired—languid.

No sign of languid with Jack. In fact, his eyes, still on Sam, were twinkling at her, as if they shared a secret joke. Twinkling, and once again firing all her nerves to skittering delight.

The word 'busking' had got Pete started, and he was now telling Jack the places he considered prime spots, so perhaps Jack hadn't noticed her reaction, although the way he looked at her suggested he might not need to notice. That the 'being as one with someone' thing was working for him as well.

'Though, unless you can sing, old mate, I don't know what you're going to do!'

'Who's going to sing? Can we all join in? It's ages since we've had a family singalong.'

Henry poked his head around the doorjamb and Sam hoped only she heard Pete's muffled groan. No matter what the outcome between herself and Henry, she didn't want him hurt or upset by her irrepressible brothers.

'I thought you said he was contagious,' Henry continued. 'Should you be in there, Peter? Sitting close to him like that?' There was a pause, then he added in disapproving tones, 'He doesn't look too sick to me.'

'Hi, Henry!' Pete broke into whatever else he might have been going to say. 'This is my friend…' He paused, then said, 'Jack. Jack, Henry Stable.'

'I won't come in and shake hands,' Henry said, giving Jack a little wave. 'I do have a tendency to catch things, don't I, Sam? Why, only at Christmas I had a nasty bout of flu and the poor darling had to spend her few days off nursing me.'

The words reminded Sam why she'd given in to Henry's demand that she name a 'decision' day. He *had* been sick, and her tender heart had pitied him.

'And if we're going out to dinner, Sam, you should be getting ready.'

Sam swung to face him.

'Henry, I'm working nights. I go on duty at ten and I have to fix dinner for—for the boys.'

She saw the disappointment in Henry's dark eyes.

'But today's the day,' he said reproachfully.

'And we'll do our own dinner. Even feed the invalid,' Pete assured her. He gave a huge grin and waggled his eyebrows at her. 'After all, if today's the day…' he added, in a stagey whisper.

Sam glared at him, but knew there was no way out. Ignoring the invalid, who was protesting that he didn't need looking after but whose eyes held a different kind of pain, she turned back to Henry.

'OK. See if you can get a late booking at Two Small Rooms, and I'll go from there to work. Change at the hospital.'

'I'll get the number for you,' Pete said, showing a rare concern for Henry.

Which left Jack and Sam alone in the spare room.

'Today's the day for what?' he asked quietly, and a sense of futility washed over her.

She shrugged it off, pretending she didn't care.

Even tried a small smile.

'Decisions,' she said.

'Decisions?' He repeated the word with an incredulity it didn't deserve. 'What kind of decision is he demanding you make?'

Tiredness had joined the futility, but as her patient's voice was getting louder, and would be heard all through the house if it continued to rise, she moved closer.

'He's not demanding anything,' she muttered. 'In fact, he's never demanded. That's probably one of the problems.'

And you shouldn't be discussing Henry with a stranger, her conscience told her. Though perhaps Jack being a stranger made him the perfect confidant.

'Henry expects, and you *know* he'll be disappointed if you don't meet those expectations. And he's kind and good so you don't like disappointing him.'

Jack groaned.

'I must be sicker than I thought. I've relapsed into the fever again. Not one word of what you've said makes sense.'

Sam sat down on the edge of the bed, drawn to the stray she had to give back, no matter how she felt about him.

'It doesn't make much sense to me either,' she said gloomily. 'I thought it did. I thought, eventually, I'd probably marry Henry. I mean, no one else ever turned up whom I liked better, so I thought—'

'That he'd do?' Incredulous didn't begin to describe his tones this time. 'That's preposterous, Sam Abbot. A beautiful, vibrant, funny, caring woman like you, settling for someone who'd ''do''? Someone who's about as exciting as rice pudding?'

The description, apt though it might be, negated the warmth from the nice things he'd said and Sam stood up, wanting to distance herself from Jack, and from her own disloyalty.

'You don't know Henry, so don't you criticise him!'

Jack caught her hand and pulled her back down, closer to him this time.

'No, I don't, and I apologise,' he said, looking deep into her eyes and sending silent messages that ran like tiny rivulets of fire along her nerves. 'He's undoubtedly a most worthy man to have attracted so fine a woman as you.'

Sam wanted to protest, or at least scoff, but something in his voice, his touch, the blueness of his eyes, held her silent.

'But what of love, Sam? What of passion, and delight, and taking that voyage of discovery into your innermost feelings with a person to whom you are truly attracted? What if, somewhere, there's one person in the world who's meant for you alone? One person with whom you could become truly, vividly alive?'

She made herself focus on his wedding ring, using it to blot out the insidious treachery of his words.

'What if I don't meet him?' she said bluntly, denying that she already had. 'I mean, what's the odds of it happening? For anyone? Five million to one? Fifty million to one?'

She knew he was watching her. Could feel his gaze burning into her skin. But she guessed her own eyes might betray the sadness she was feeling, so she looked away, and this time when she stood up she stepped back, out of reach.

Out of touching distance.

He said nothing, but as she walked through the door she imagined she heard his voice.

Imagined he'd said, 'Say no, Sam.'

CHAPTER EIGHT

'PROBLEMS in paradise,' Pete whispered to Sam as she walked into the kitchen.

He nodded towards Henry who was on the phone, but from the tenor of the conversation he wasn't speaking to a restaurant.

And from the way he slammed the phone back onto the receiver, there was someone else currently receiving a buzzing in his or her ear.

'Did you know hospitals won't take a patient without a doctor's say-so?' he demanded.

The question made no sense at all.

'They're not respite centres, Henry,' Pete, who apparently did know what was going on, said. 'You can't just drop off Aunt Maud when you're tired of her, or any Tom, Dick or Jack.'

Light dawned.

'You were phoning a hospital about Jack?' Sam knew she sounded as disbelieving as she felt. 'Why? He's a lot better. And Dr Charlton's coming up to see him in a day or two, but that's because he's interested in dengue.'

'Don't say the word!' Pete told her. 'That's what set him off!'

'Well, you shouldn't have him here,' Henry said reprovingly. 'A total stranger. Peter tells me you found him in the bush and brought him home. I can't believe you'd be so irresponsible, Samantha.'

'Boy, you must be in real trouble to be getting the Samantha treatment!'

Sean's comment preceded him into the room. He ranged himself beside his sister and nodded to their new guest.

'Henry.'

It was an acknowledgment but not a greeting.

'So, what's the fuss?'

He directed the question at Pete, but it was Henry who replied.

'I was telling Sam the man should be in hospital.'

'Jack! His name's Jack,' Sam said, irrationally irritated by Henry's words.

'Actually, his name's not Jack. We just call him that,' Sean explained, and Sam wondered if this was how the world would end, not with a bang but with total confusion.

'Stop right now!' she commanded, holding up both her hands. 'Let's not take this conversation any further. Henry, did you make a booking? Shouldn't you be changing? I certainly should be. Sean, you might check on Jack. I think he'd like assistance with a shave. Pete, you're in charge of dinner. You offered, remember. Now I'm going to get dressed.'

She hustled back to her bedroom, anxious to get an assortment of clothes and the other things she'd need shifted into Gran's room before Henry returned. She showered in Gran's *en suite*, and dressed in a slinky navy shift dress that clung to her body like a second skin.

She'd bought it to wear out with Henry when she'd been at home for Christmas, but his summer flu had put a stop to any frivolity.

'Wow!'

Pete's comment when she returned to the kitchen made her flush with pleasure. Her brothers were more likely to tell her when she didn't measure up than when she did.

Henry's compliment, however, left her feeling slightly flat.

'I like your hair brushed up like that,' he said, coming to stand beside her and slide his arm around her waist.

As she had fluffed her short hair out and up so it took on a nimbus effect around her face, she had to give him points for noticing.

Sean came in, repeated the 'Wow' his brother had used, grinned at his sister, then wandered through to the family room beyond the open kitchen to turn on the television.

'Oh, good,' Henry said. 'We can catch the early news before we go.' He released Sam to hurry forward, then perch on the edge of a chair as if the evening's disclosure of death, disaster and rising interest rates was of prime importance.

So much for slinky dresses, Sam thought, but she, too, moved forward, leaning against the bench that divided the two rooms and watching the small screen.

Pictures of war-torn villages in eastern Europe, an accident on the South-East freeway, interest rates going up— when weren't they?

Behind her she heard the click of crutches on the wooden floor in the hall and guessed that Jack was making his way towards the kitchen.

Henry was explaining why interest rate rises were good for foreign investment, Sean was baiting him and no one was taking much notice of the news when a photo of a man filled the screen.

'That's Grant Hudson,' she said, pointing at the screen. 'He's a new neurosurgeon at the hospital.'

'That's our Jack!'

Sean's words came out at the same time as hers, mingling with and muddling both sentences.

'Well, whoever he is, the police want to contact him in connection with a bank robbery,' Henry said in his sternest voice. 'Though I don't know why Sean would think the scruffy individual you have in there looks anything like that man!' He added the rider as the picture was again flashed across the screen.

'That's me!' Jack's voice came from behind her.

'Well,' Henry snorted. 'Fancy admitting he's a bank robber.'

His voice held so much satisfaction that Sam wanted to hit him, but instead she turned towards her 'stray' and nearly fell over when a handsome, clean-shaven, but slightly too thin face presented itself to her.

'What do you think? A bit patchy, with the white skin underneath where the beard was, and your stitches could have been neater, but it's better, isn't it?'

The rueful smile accompanying the words tugged at the strings that held her heart in place. The paleness where the beard had been made him look vulnerable somehow, though she knew from the grim way he'd suffered pain as they'd struggled out of the rainforest that vulnerable didn't fit in this man's description.

'A lot better,' she managed to say, as her brain struggled to make sense of the auditory and sensory messages bombarding it. And her eyes remained riveted on Jack's face!

Henry was out of his chair and walking purposefully towards the phone.

'I'll contact the police.'

'No!'

Sam's cry escaped from deep within her—and earned her a withering glare from Henry.

'Don't be ridiculous!' he told her. 'You can't keep harbouring a criminal.'

'It's best he phones them.' Jack's deep voice was pitched so only she could hear it, and it dropped even lower when he added, 'I'd have done it myself if the sight of my rescuer in that sexy, slinky, should-be-X-rated little number hadn't stolen my breath.'

'Well, at least that proves you're a Tom, not a Jack.' Pete spoke before she could fully assimilate the compliment she'd wanted earlier from Henry. Her brother held out his hand in a gesture of welcome—of acceptance. 'How do you do, Tom Hudson?'

'Tom Hudson?' The name penetrated the blur in her brain. 'Is that what they said his name is? Then Grant is your brother.'

She turned to face Jack—or was he Tom?

'I found Grant last night. He *is* a brain surgeon. Grant Hudson. He's just started at my hospital. He did the surgery. I dropped the Kerrison punch when I saw his eyes.'

Tom rested one hand on her shoulder.

'Calm down,' he said gently. 'We'll sort it all out.'

She covered his hand with her own, and managed to find a smile.

'Even if you're in jail for bank robbery?'

The answering smile, spreading his newly revealed lips wide and gleaming in his eyes, made her want to cry.

'Even if I'm in jail,' he said, making it sound special— like a promise she knew he'd keep.

Which was ridiculous, because now they knew who he was he definitely had to go back. There was still Jocelyn, and that wedding ring!

'The police are sending someone right away,' Henry announced, looking suspiciously at Tom, as if expecting him to make a run for it.

'Good.' The newly christened Tom made it sound as if nothing could have pleased him more. 'Let's sit down while we wait. I don't know about you lot, but all this standing around makes my arms ache.'

Pete and Sean both laughed at the weak joke, but Sean paused by Sam and slipped an arm around her shoulders.

'I actually listened to that news report,' he said quietly. 'The car used as a getaway vehicle was traced to Tom, but he'd have to be a totally dumb robber to use his own BMW in a bank heist. And Jack, or even Tom, in that scenario doesn't work for me!'

She smiled at this brotherly reassurance, although why he thought she needed it was another question.

As she watched Tom settle himself into a chair at the big kitchen table, another thought occurred to her.

'Does knowing your name help?' she asked. 'Does it feel real?'

He grinned.

'Actually, the Tom part had already come back to me. Some time in the night I remember protesting to the twins that I was Tom, not Jack.'

The words fell into a moment of silence, and echoed there.

'You remembered who you were last night?' She spun to face her brothers. 'You two knew?'

'He didn't remember much, sis,' Pete said quickly.

'Couldn't remember why he was where he was, or how he'd got there, or even how he came to be in Australia,' Sean added. 'He was sick, remember, delirious. We could hardly take much notice of him, now, could we?'

Sam pushed back her chair and stood up.

'Don't we have a dinner engagement, Henry?'

Poor Henry looked stunned—well, more stunned. He'd done the ordinary stunned much earlier.

'We can't go— The police— They'll want to ask you questions. It will make you look guilty if you run away.'

Sam wondered, briefly, just how much anger it would take to make the top fly off her head.

'They can follow me to the restaurant,' she announced. 'They can question me at work. It's not as if I'm fleeing the country, Henry!'

She stalked from the room, not caring if he followed. Then she remembered something else and turned back, fixing Tom Hudson with her steely stare this time.

'You can contact your brother through the hospital. And I know he'll be able to put you in touch with Jocelyn.' Then something which hadn't clicked earlier in the day synapsed in her head. 'By the way, her surname's Milson, not Hudson. Your mistress, perhaps?'

And on that note she departed, detouring briefly into Gran's bedroom to retrieve her handbag and uniform, then marching through the front door, down the steps and out to her car.

'We really shouldn't go. It's irresponsible, Sam. Those brothers of yours are likely to help him escape,' Henry babbled as he followed her, his hands fluttering in front of him as if conducting his protest.

Sam turned to him.

'Oh, Henry, grow up, for heaven's sake! Do you honestly believe the man's a bank robber?'

'Why else would he grow a beard?'

Sam closed her eyes and counted to ten. Then added another five for luck.

'There are any number of reasons a man might grow a beard, but if it was solely for the purpose of robbing banks, then wouldn't he starve to death before it got long enough? Wouldn't putting on a false one be easier?'

The look Henry gave her didn't bode well for the evening ahead but, considering the decision she'd finally reached, the one she had to relay to him this very evening, it wasn't likely to be a bundle of laughs anyway.

He strode across to his car, which was parked behind

hers in the half-circle of the drive, and used his remote to
unlock the doors.

'I'll take my car,' Sam said, when she realised he was
heading diligently towards the passenger side to open the
door for her. 'That way I can go straight on to work.'

'I could drive you to work,' he said stiffly.

'And come back at five to collect me? I wouldn't ask
that of you, Henry.'

He slammed the door shut and did his stiff-legged walk
back around the bonnet.

The evening was deteriorating faster than she'd expected.
Though she had to laugh when he started the engine and
planted his foot on the accelerator, revving furiously, then
reversed back along the drive, stopping only when a loud
blast of a car horn and the crunch of metal told him he'd
run into something.

Something with red lights flashing on the top of it.

The noise brought the twins to the verandah.

'Shouldn't you be watching the dangerous criminal?
Making sure he doesn't escape?' she asked them, though
most of her attention was on Henry all but prostrating himself in apology to the police.

'Henry?' Sean asked, and Sam nodded.

'You're better off without him, sis,' Pete said. 'Tell him
tonight. We know we shouldn't interfere but, honestly, he's
not the man for you. Surely meeting Jack—Tom—has
made you realise that.'

'He's married,' Sam reminded him, knowing he'd understand exactly which 'he' she meant.

'But there'll be other Jacks,' Sean told her. 'There always were, but you were too blind to see. Too loyal to
some stupid idea our mother and his dreamed up when you
were little. Henry's a decent guy but, Sam, if you really
loved him, would you keep putting off going home? Keep

taking more and more courses as an excuse to stay in Brisbane?'

'You're always telling us to grow up,' Pete added. 'So how about taking your own advice?'

Sam shook her head in disbelief.

'And how often do you two discuss my future? How long did it take you to work out my life for me?'

The pair grinned at her.

'Actually, it was Gran,' they chorused, then Sean explained. 'She's the one who first pointed out Henry wasn't right for you. Said if you loved the man you'd have married him years ago.'

'She can talk!' sniffed Sam, then she turned her attention to the drama in the drive. The police car had backed away from Henry's big Ford with only a minimum of grinding noises. The Ford's back bumper dropped to the ground, but the police car seemed to be intact, although one headlight pointed skywards.

'I'll cancel your dinner booking and order pizza for us all,' Pete suggested, and Sean followed him into the house.

Sam remained at the bottom of the steps. After the comments she'd made to Tom Hudson, she didn't particularly want to face him again. And facing Henry, who, no doubt, blamed her intransigence for the accident, would be nearly as upsetting.

Perhaps *she* could rob a bank! It was about the only way things could get worse.

Or she could go to work early. Escape them all. The road was clear in front of her car. All she had to do was get in and drive away.

The inner relief she felt as she considered this cowardly way out was so great that the solution seemed miraculous.

'I'll be at work if the police need me,' she called to

Henry, adding a deceitful verisimilitude to the statement by waving her mobile in the air.

Then, knowing he'd argue, and suspecting the police might object if they realised who she was, she slipped into the car and took off.

Carefully!

But as she joined the stream of evening traffic, she began to worry about her stray.

If he couldn't remember anything beyond his name, how could he convince the police he had nothing to do with the robbery?

What if the police arrested him?

Who would stand up for him? Explain who he was?

It was not yet seven. Perhaps Grant Hudson would still be at the hospital. From the blank way Tom had reacted to Grant Hudson's name, he was unlikely to phone him. There must be a Swiss-cheese-type hole in his memory where his brother should be.

But if the police had been in touch with Grant, or other members of Tom's family, he must be worrying. And even if he wasn't, surely it was his duty to stand by his brother?

She'd page him, that would be best. If his patient was still in the ICU, he'd not think anything of it.

Though if he was at home and came in specially in answer to a page, he'd be furious!

Better if she tried his office.

Plotting how best to meet the surgeon occupied her on the drive to the hospital, but as she walked along the long corridor where the doctors had their suites, her shaky knees suggested that having a nice quiet cup of coffee and a toasted sandwich in the cafeteria might be an infinitely better idea.

Scorn for such cowardice forced her on.

She found the door with the new nameplate screwed at

eye-level, and was lifting a hand to knock when a voice said, 'May I help you?'

The words startled her so much that she dropped her uniform and, bending to retrieve it, knocked heads with the man who'd crept up behind her.

'Oh, no! Not the clumsy nurse!' he muttered as recognition lit his so-familiar blue eyes. 'Is this what people call stalking? What's with you, woman? What do you want of me?'

He sounded so like Jack—Tom—that Sam almost smiled, but his eyes weren't soft and twinkly. In fact, they were fixed on her with a ferocious intensity.

'It's about your brother. About Tom, if that's his name. I guess it must be, although we called him Jack. He didn't know, you see. Still doesn't remember a lot of things, I don't think he remembers you, it's the Swiss cheese thing, although his memory's returning so quickly he might remember you by now. But the police are there, and if he can't tell them where he was when the robbery took place, and they arrest him—'

She stopped as long slim fingers seized her arm and ushered her through the now-open door.

'What do you know of my brother?' Grant Hudson demanded, when he'd shut the door. He was now leaning against it, effectively trapping her inside what must be the dragon's office.

'I found a man—in the bush. He fell down a cliff, broke his ankle and suffered enough of a head injury to cause amnesia. He didn't know who he was or where he was or how he came to be there.'

She realised how ridiculous it all sounded, and added, 'He did remember his brother was a brain surgeon.' The disbelief she could read in Grant Hudson's eyes soared off the Richter scale.

'It's true.' She protested against the unspoken accusation. 'I know it sounds so off-the-planet you must think I'm crazy, but that's exactly what happened. Anyway, I got him out and took him to hospital but they refused to keep him and so I took him home.'

The disbelief had nothing on the scorn that now took its place.

'You're telling me you picked up an injured stranger in the bush—and, believe me, if it was my brother there's no way a little thing like you would have got him out—then took him home because the hospital wouldn't keep him?'

Sam had no other words with which to convince him, so she nodded. Then remembered why she'd decided to find this man.

'But now the police are there. They're accusing him of bank robbery. You'll have to see them. Explain about the amnesia. Tell them who he is, and what he does.'

Scorn turned to understanding. Even sympathy.

'Sit down,' Grant Hudson said, ushering her towards a chair. And in the gentle touch he laid on her elbow, in the look in his eyes, she read the conclusion he must have reached.

That she was mad. Demented. Whacky as a loon!

Great! The police were carting his brother off to jail and he was working out how to get her locked up as well.

A light tap on the door interrupted whatever he'd been about to do or say, and he opened it to usher in a tall, slim brunette, stunningly attired in a black designer suit, sheer black stockings and four-inch heels.

Sam felt a twinge of pity for her simple, slinky dress having to come face to face with so much magnificence.

'Really, Grant!' the newcomer said, her voice strident with annoyance. 'I accepted a serious operation as an ex-

cuse last night, but to stand me up two nights in a row.
Taking things rather too far.'

Sam caught a look of helplessness in the expressive blue
eyes that swung her way, but the man rallied, smoothly
introducing the two women.

'Jocelyn, this is—'

'Sam Abbot,' Sam said helpfully, although she doubted
whether knowing her own name would convince him of
her sanity.

'Sam Abbot,' he repeated. 'Jocelyn Milson. My brother's
fiancée.'

'Your brother's ex-fiancée,' Jocelyn corrected. 'He's finished as far as I'm concerned. Honestly, Grant, I thought
if I let him go off on that mad whim to Sumatra it would
get the monkey business out of his system for ever. But did
he return a chastened man? No way! Back he comes, home
less than a day, and he disappears without a word.'

'To rob a bank, apparently,' Grant murmured, and Sam
caught him reassessing her.

'You're just as bad as he is!' Jocelyn stormed. 'Making
a joke of everything! Well, I'm going to the restaurant. If
you want to join me when you've finished dallying with—'

'Sam Abbot,' Sam said helpfully.

'Her, you can join me!'

She walked out and slammed the door behind her, leaving so brittle a silence in her wake that Sam had to hold
back the giggle that threatened to escape her.

'He's married, you know,' she said to Grant, then realised the reassessment wasn't going to be helped by piling
more and more shocks on the man.

'Married?'

'The man I found. The one who looks like you. You *are*
identical twins, aren't you? He's wearing a wedding ring.'

Grant Hudson groaned and held his head in his hands.

'Married! That's *all* I need! Now I not only have to tell Jocelyn he's lost his memory, and can't remember anything about her, but that somewhere along his erratic way he's managed to get married.'

'Actually, he does remember Jocelyn,' Sam said, pleased to find her companion seemed more receptive of her story now. 'At least, he remembers her name. I don't think he knows about an engagement. Though, perhaps if it's off now, as she said, he won't have to worry about it.'

'If only!' Grant sighed, then his frown returned. 'I can't believe I'm discussing this as if any of your preposterous story could possibly be true.'

'And I can't believe you'd be so stubborn about believing it! I thought you'd be pleased to know he was all right,' Sam told him. 'Well, more or less all right. Did I tell you about the broken ankle? And the dengue fever?'

'Serves him right!' Grant said fiercely. 'He'll have a sore ear as well when I'm done with telling him exactly what I think of him. Of all the irresponsible, delayed adolescent behaviour— Did you say dengue fever? It's not haemorrhagic, is it?'

Sam saw his concern for his brother in his eyes, and felt it in the way he seized her arm again.

But nothing tingled along her nerves. No rivulets of fire darted down her veins.

How could one man do it to her, yet this man's touch, this *identical* man's touch, have no effect?

'Why don't you go and see him?' she said gently. 'You must be due to go off duty. I'll give you my address. It's not far.'

His pager intervened before he could reply and he snatched it off his belt and read the message.

'Perhaps later,' he muttered, walking through to the next room and returning with a clean white coat. 'But right now, if you're due on duty, it's all hands on deck. Bus accident on the freeway. Injured coming into the major hospitals. They'll be calling in extra theatre staff, so as you're here already…' He left the rest of the sentence unsaid. Everyone knew what a freeway accident could entail.

She didn't have time to tell him she wasn't officially theatre staff any more, and that she'd probably be needed in the ICU tonight anyway.

He'd whisked away, but before she left she wrote Tom's name, Tom Hudson, followed by her name, address and phone number on a piece of paper, and left it in the centre of the dragon's perfectly tidy desk.

CHAPTER NINE

KNOWING it could be a long and arduous night ahead, Sam hurried down to the cafeteria first and bought a couple of packets of sandwiches. She then reported to the ICU, where the evening shift charge nurse, Nancy Reynolds, greeted her with relief.

'You're two hours early, so eat first,' Nancy suggested, when she saw the sandwich packs in Sam's hand. 'Use the tearoom. Make yourself a cuppa. The injured are only just arriving. They'll need to be assessed in A and E, then prioritised. I've staff who are willing to stay on from this shift to prepare our spare beds. We'll be taking anyone needing life support, and I'm assuming we'll get a few more as post-ops.'

'But you've limited space,' Sam reminded her.

'Six beds—actually, seven if we count the infectious room. But I doubt we'll need more. Other hospitals are involved, and with any luck most of the injuries will be minor.'

The buzz of a muted phone took the charge nurse back to the desk. Sam listened to one end of the conversation and guessed that things were hotting up.

'Might have guessed this would happen. You're wanted up in Theatre,' Nancy told her. 'When you get in, Frankie said, so go eat first. She was phoning from home. She's been paged to come in early.' She paused then added, 'And perhaps put on a uniform. You'll give any men up there heart failure if you go upstairs in that slinky outfit.'

Sam closed her eyes and shook her head, unable to believe she hadn't given a thought to what she'd been wearing when she'd rushed into the hospital in search of Grant Hudson.

She ate a sandwich as she changed into her uniform, although she'd be getting out of it soon enough, then had a long drink of water and dug in her handbag for her mobile. Phoned home.

Sean answered.

'How's everything going?' she whispered to him, although no one could hear her at this end.

'Fine!' he whispered back. 'The cops are gone. They didn't like the story, suspicious blighters that they are, but they didn't take Tom away, which is the good news.'

'If the police are gone you can stop that silly whispering,' she told him crossly. 'What's the bad news?'

'He says he has to go anyway. Says he'll have to find this brother you mentioned and stay with him until he gets better. Pete and I have tied him to the bed and locked the room but I reckon Henry will not only set him free but drive him somewhere if we're not careful.'

Unable to voice any of what she was thinking—in fact, unable to sort it into coherence in her mind—Sam said, 'His brother's busy. It's panic stations here!' And disconnected. Let someone else listen to buzzing noises.

Sally Cochrane greeted her as she pushed through the swing doors into the clean corridor at the back of the bank of theatres.

'Great. The reserves have landed. I've an eighteen-year-old with an acute subdural haematoma coming up. CT scan showed a crescent-shaped mass. We'll operate to remove the clot and hope there's not too much underlying brain damage. You can scrub.'

Eighteen was too young to die, Sam thought, and superstitiously crossed her fingers.

'It's less than three hours since the accident,' Sally continued. 'Four hours is our optimum window of opportunity.'

She disappeared into what was now the doctors' changing room.

The patient was already in Theatre when Sam wheeled in the trolley with a sterilised neuro bundle on it. The anaesthetist, a woman Sam didn't recognise behind her mask, had the monitors set up behind the table so Sally would have good access to the patient's head. The carefully measured fluid he would have been given earlier had been replaced by full blood.

Sally and an intern came in, then Sam realised that it wasn't an intern. It was Grant Hudson.

And they were arguing.

'We've a time frame, Dr Cochrane,' the man said. 'If that clot grows big enough to displace the brain stem from the midline, even move it slightly, the patient's outcome will be disastrous.'

'But if the vein is still bleeding and we don't tie it off, the outcome's equally bad,' Sally suggested.

'Our job includes tying it off,' Grant Hudson said coldly.

Burr-hole surgery versus craniotomy, Sam guessed. Since she'd been working in Theatre, more and more surgery was performed through very small holes—keyholes—which certainly shortened the patient's recovery period.

Grant's eyes swept the room and found Sam.

'Can you set up the microscope?' he demanded.

Sam bit back a sarcastic retort and stuck with nodding in agreement. Sally was already drilling the first burr hole. She would drill another then join them to provide a 'window' into the skull.

Once a section of the hard bone was cut through and hinged back, a flap of the dura, a tough, inelastic membrane directly beneath the skull, would be cut and held back, so the surgeons could see the space beneath it.

'Subdural haematomas are rare in young people,' Grant said. 'Even in vehicle accidents. More likely to get them in an older person, often from a low-impact injury like a fall.'

He used a conversational tone but Sam realised he was directing the words at Sally, reinforcing things she probably already knew. To keep her calm? Did he suspect she couldn't perform under pressure?

Though what was yesterday's spinal operation, if not pressure?

The man's attitude was a mystery.

Handing Sally another instrument, Sam decided she was pleased she'd moved on from theatre work. She'd always enjoyed neurosurgery work, which was usually carried out in Theatre Five, but the atmosphere in neuro was deteriorating fast.

Frankie came in as Grant asked for the microscope.

'I'll set it up,' she said to Sally. 'You stay where you are.'

She swung the arm of the microscope across the table so the two sets of binocular eyepieces were directly above the surgeons' heads. The instrument was draped in sterile sheer plastic sheeting, so the surgeons could pull down the eyepieces and operate the controls without contamination.

As the surgeon adjusted the microscope to enlarge the area of damage, Sam watched on a video screen. Using a microscopic suctioning tool, the blood from the clot was removed. No one spoke, although the hum of the various machines provided the usual background noise.

The two surgeons stared into the wound, while the rest of the staff studied the monitor for signs that the torn vein was still bleeding.

'Looks like it's sealed itself,' Sally muttered.

Sam waited for the new man to say, 'I told you so.'

He didn't, which raised him a millimetre in her estimation.

He pushed the microscope out of the way and stood back while Sally began to stitch the dura back together.

'Where can I reach my brother?' he said, turning to Sam who was busy handing sutures to the resident.

'I left the number on your secretary's desk,' she told him, then she checked the big-faced clock on the theatre wall.

'It's after one, you can't phone now!' she told him. As ever, she was surprised by how fast time passed in an operating theatre.

Grant Hudson muttered something that sounded like, 'Beset by bloody argumentative women.' And walked out.

Sam heaved a sigh of relief.

At least she hadn't dropped anything.

'Brother?'

Frankie and Sally both asked the question, but there was no way Sam was going to explain.

'Want to engrave "Life's a bitch" on the inside of the bone flap?' she asked Sally instead, waving the electrocautery knife at the surgeon.

She saw Sally's eyes twinkle.

'With my luck, the wound would become infected, his lordship would order the bone flap removed and I'd be caught!'

The silly conversation, based on a true story one of the visiting neurosurgeons had told, reduced the level of stress in the room, and the fact that the patient had remained stable throughout the operation gave them hope that he'd make a good recovery.

'Although,' Frankie reminded her as they changed into clean scrubs, 'if he's hit his head with enough force to rupture veins beneath the dura, he's likely to have caused damage to his brain anyway.'

Contusion, the bruising caused when the soft brain, propelled forwards and then backwards in the sudden deceleration of an accident, crashed against the hardness of the skull, could leave the victim permanently disabled.

Once again, Sam crossed her fingers.

The phone on the wall bleated a summons. Frankie answered it, said yes several times, then hung up and turned to Sam.

'No more urgent head injuries. Apparently there are a few "wait and watch" cases but right now we've an orthopaedic patient coming up. Broken femur with damage to the femoral artery so they don't want to wait. I'll scrub this one. You circulate.'

Sam finished dressing, already thinking of the different instruments the orthopaedic surgeon would need. Power-operated tools akin to a carpenter's, plus nails and screws and wires. She set a general surgery bundle on the trolley for repairs to the artery, then a second parcel of orthopaedic requirements. Depending on the wound, and its severity, the surgeon could choose either a closed or open reduction of the injury. If blood vessels were at risk, he might go for open, but who could ever read their minds?

She grabbed a third parcel and put it on the bottom shelf, then congratulated herself because she felt she'd covered all eventualities.

The speed at which the next patient arrived suggested that people were lined up outside the door.

'Leave that with me and help the doctors glove up,' Frankie said

'It's a madhouse down there,' Don Jacobs, the orthopaedic registrar, announced as he came into the scrub room.

'Why seat belts aren't mandatory in all buses I'll never know.'

He scrubbed as he talked, complaining about the drain on resources such major accidents caused. His assistant, a resident Sam knew by sight, hung on every word.

Silly woman's in love with him, Sam thought, then something in her chest gave a little kick and she had to summon all her mental power to deny such a thing had happened to her.

'Shall we go?' Don asked, when Sam had gloved his upheld hands. He turned to the woman and winked. 'Together into the great unknown?'

Sam retracted her 'silly woman' thought when she saw the softness in his eyes. He might well be just as much in love, she decided. In which case, it was nice. Two people with similar interests.

'And you're going soft in the head!' she muttered into her mask as she followed the pair into the theatre.

'Because there is involvement with the artery and the X-rays show a muscle mass interposing between the ends of the bone, I'm going to open the leg and expose the break,' Don told the collected staff. An intern had appeared while Sam had been out of the theatre. He must have walked out of the scrub room by the theatre door as she'd gone in from the corridor.

He was new to surgery if his anxiety to keep out of the way was any indication. 'Once the bones are reamed,' Don continued, 'I'll put a nail through from the greater trochanter to the fracture site, and drive it home through to the lower fragment.'

Sam shuddered, remembering why she was glad she'd never been permanently appointed to the main orthopedic theatre.

Frankie activated the exflow, which set up a curtain of

sterile air around the operating table. For joint replace-
ments, the surgeons and scrub nurse would also wear body
exhaust gowns, to further eliminate contamination of the
wound. With emergency surgery, such niceties were set
aside. It was more important to keep blood flowing into his
toes.

As Don worked, he talked—about the accident, the
wound, what he was doing and why.

'Chap should be able to leave hospital in a week, and be
weight-bearing in a fortnight,' he told the intern, who'd
been beckoned closer to cauterise small bleeders and was
looking slightly green.

Carefully, the protrusion of muscle was returned to its
correct alignment, the artery, which had been constricted
by the movement, was settled back into place, and the task
of reaming the ends of the bone and then aligning their
cavities began.

'Hammer time!' Frankie whispered to Sam, as the nail
was driven into position.

Then the wound was closed, layer upon layer of muscle
and connective tissue carefully stitched back together, and
finally the skin.

'Now Anne and I have done the tricky stuff, you can do
this bit,' Don told the intern, who almost visibly pulled
himself together then began inserting sutures neatly into the
internal edges of the wound.

The senior surgeon waited only long enough to see that
the young doctor was capable of closing, then he walked
away.

'I hope I don't see any of you later,' he remarked. 'But
I wouldn't bet on it.'

The patient was wheeled through to Recovery, and Sam
began the job of cleaning up. The soiled 'sharps' were already in their sealed container and the reusable instruments

and drapes would go to the hospital sterilisation unit. She took them out to the disposal room, checking carefully that no blade or needle had been left among the instruments to cause injury to staff further down the line.

'Transplant team wants this theatre set up for them,' Frankie told her, and Sam felt the sense of sadness such news always brought. Though, if the operation was successful, one person would have a second chance to lead a normal life, it also meant they'd lost the fight with another patient.

Like the Old Testament retribution of a life for a life.

Setting up for transplant surgery was complicated as machines were used so the blood could bypass whichever organ was being transplanted.

'We'll have the donor,' Frankie added. 'The recipient will be next door.'

Sam helped her move the appropriate equipment into place, although she knew she'd probably be off duty before surgery began. Cross-matching blood, typing, preparing both the patient and the donor—it all took time and it was already after four.

If every theatre in the hospital had been as busy, then the ICU and the wards would be bulging at the seams.

'I'd better check in at the ICU,' she told Frankie when the senior nurse suggested a cup of coffee.

'You'll get stuck there if you do,' Frankie warned. 'Our femur won't go there, but the haematoma will. And who knows how many other patients they've admitted?'

Sam grinned at her.

'They were setting up extra rooms before I came to Theatre, so I should at least check on who's gone into them.'

'Foolish woman!' Frankie said, waving her away with a languid hand.

ICU was as busy as she'd imagined and Wendy greeted her with relief.

'Can you take your head-injury man? He's just down from Recovery. They must be making space for someone else to send him as early as this.'

Sam decided not to mention the transplant. Post-op transplant patients were very dicey, and needed extra-careful watching for the slightest sign of anything going wrong. And even with the up-to-date equipment, catching trouble early was still partly instinctive.

Her patient arrived as she was deciding she'd prefer the head injury to a transplant victim. He was comatose, but she knew that had possibly been induced in order to keep him quiet and give his damaged brain time to heal.

'You know what you're watching for?' Wendy asked as they removed the portable monitors and ventilator and connected him to their own. 'Any change in his neurological status. For that we rely on observations as well as what the screen says.'

They raised the head of the bed to help reduce his intra-cranial pressure. This could cause a secondary insult to the brain, as could any imbalance of nutrients or oxygen in the blood.

Grant Hudson came in as they finished settling the young man, who now had a name—William Crichton.

The surgeon took in the wires and tubes connecting William to monitors and fluids, then picked up the file and wrote for several minutes.

'Call me immediately if there's any sign of deterioration,' he told Wendy. 'Particularly if there's an increase in his ICP.'

His eyes shifted and met Sam's, and she almost smiled as she saw an unmistakable double take!

'Are there only two of you, or did you come as triplets? Or, heaven forbid, quads?'

Wendy stared at him, and Sam hid a smile as she replied, 'That's rich, coming from a twin! There's just me. I'm floating.'

He raised his eyes towards the ceiling and groaned.

'I must be getting old. Can't take these all-nighters any more.' Then he paused and added, 'By floating, I assume you mean moving around in different areas.'

Sam nodded, although she'd barely heard the words, too busy noticing little differences between this man and Tom.

'Which means you must be about to go off duty,' he added, checking his watch and nodding to where nurses in fresh, clean uniforms signalled a change of shift.

'I'll stay as long as I'm needed here,' Sam told him.

Then Wendy ruined everything by saying, 'No. Now we've got him settled you can go. Go on. I've extra staff coming on for the day shift. I'll see you tonight, though, and I'll tell Theatre you're no longer floating. You're mine.'

Sam grinned at the possessiveness in Wendy's voice, then realised the surgeon was still with them.

'Well, come on,' he said, opening the door and waving her towards it. 'I'll drive you home.'

Behind her, Sam thought she heard Wendy whisper, 'Fast worker.' But that didn't make much sense.

Neither did Grant Hudson driving her home.

'I've got my car. You can follow me,' she told him.

'Nonsense. We need to talk. I can't talk to you if you're in your car and I'm in mine. Wait here!'

She could continue to argue, or she could go along with it. Get one of the boys to drive her to work tonight.

And while giving in to his imperious demands went

against the grain, it *would* be an opportunity to find out more about Jack—Tom!

He parked her beside the nurses' station while he stepped around the counter to look at the monitors. The day shift charge nurse, Ian Wheeler, had arrived. He'd trained with Sam, but it had been a long time since their paths had crossed.

'Hi, beautiful,' he said, blowing her a kiss. 'Now you've finally made it to where the real business of this hospital happens, we'll get to work together again. That's if Wendy ever releases you from night shift.'

'*If* you don't mind!' Grant Hudson said to him, casting a disapproving look in Sam's direction.

Ian gave his attention to the impatient surgeon, but although he listened and nodded and even took a couple of notes, he found time to wink at Sam, first with his left eye, then with his right.

'And I'd get that twitch seen to,' Grant Hudson said to him, stepping out from behind the console and taking Sam by the elbow. 'Come along, Nurse Abbot.'

And, as he ushered her out of the unit, the nerves down Sam's spine suggested that every member of the staff was watching their departure, and she could all but hear the speculation that would follow when they were safely out of earshot.

'You can let go now!' Sam told him as they reached the lifts. 'I'm not going to run away. I'm as anxious to reunite you with your brother as you are to see him. Although you didn't show much enthusiasm when I tried to tell you yesterday.'

The lift arrived and an anxious-looking couple disembarked.

Grant paused to speak to them and Sam guessed they must be William's parents. The lift door closed again, but the surgeon, who'd been abrupt to the point of rudeness with her and with other staff, continued to talk quietly to these two people whose lives had been so tragically disrupted.

'What do you think?' she asked him when he returned from showing them into the unit. 'Will he make a full recovery? Could you see how much damage had been done to the brain?'

The lift came again and this time they caught it. It was half-full and Tom steered her towards the back.

'It didn't look too bad, but it's hard to tell. You could probably see a slight displacement on the monitor, but the young man is healthy and has led an active life. His general level of fitness will count in his favour.'

Sam heard a sadness in his voice and forgot his testiness.

'Why do you work in neurosurgery when so many cases are hopeless?'

He looked down into her face, his eyes, so familiar yet not known, smiling at her.

'I guess because of the ones that aren't hopeless. Or that would be if I didn't do something.' He looked away, checking the floor number, then said nothing more until they were in the basement and he was leading the way towards his car.

'But neurosurgery isn't all haematomas and aneurysms, you know. It's a lot about pain relief. You get a patient who's been in chronic pain for years and you can cure it with a simple operation—that's rewarding.'

Sam accepted his words in silence, not knowing him well enough to scoff. But in her heart she knew that such simple operations wouldn't be enough of a challenge for this man. It *was* the life-or-death stuff he would find most challenging, the so-called hopeless patients his most rewarding cases.

'Now, tell me again from the beginning,' he ordered, when Sam was buckled into his car and had given him sufficient directions to get him started in the right direction.

'Damn! We'll have to go back,' she told him, finally realising how strong his influence had been. 'I've left my handbag, street clothes, everything, at work.'

'Locked in a locker, I assume,' Grant said.

'Of course,' Sam told him.

'Then they'll be safe, won't they?' he said calmly. 'Tell me about Tom.'

She wanted to protest this bullying, insist he turn around, but there was something implacable about the man and she'd already experienced the futility of arguing with him.

Not that she intended giving in altogether.

'Where was he?' she asked. 'The way Miss Milson spoke he's been away. Was it Sumatra?'

Grant took his attention off the traffic for long enough to glance her way.

'I thought you said he had amnesia.'

'He's got holes. Seems to know some things and not others.' She remembered something else Jocelyn had said. Monkey business! 'Why was he away?'

'Bloody monkeys!' Grant said, accelerating through an orange light then slowing down again.

'I guess that's a step up from pigs as far as animals are concerned,' Sam told him, and caught another look that suggested he thought her mad.

'He's a haematologist,' Grant told her. 'Lecturer in the subject. He's been working at a major Sydney teaching hospital for many years. But in his spare time he's studied monkeys. He's got some bee in his bonnet about the antibodies in monkey blood, and their usefulness as study or monitoring tools for human research.'

'Sumatra!' Sam murmured as several bits of information

clicked into place. 'Isn't there a place in Sumatra where orang-outangs are trained to go back to the jungle?'

Grant laughed.

'Near Medan—yes. He went there years ago. In fact, every holiday during his years at university. No, the monkeys he's stuck on now are the bilou. There's a colony of them on a little island off the coast of Sumatra that's been cut off from other land for thousands of years.'

'Bilou? I've never heard of them.'

Grant half turned and smiled at her.

'Believe me, neither have most of the world's population. But apparently they live in family groups which makes them rare. They are a species of gibbon and, along with humans, are the only primates that operate this way. Other species live in packs.'

Sam was about to ask what family groups had to do with anything when she realised they'd missed a turn. By the time she'd given directions to get them back on track, they were nearly home.

'Keep going straight ahead and it's the big house on the right.'

'Big house?' Grant queried. 'It's huge. Trust Tom to fall on a woman who can offer a bit of comfort.'

Sam found the joking remark unsettling.

'He didn't fall *on* me,' she snapped. 'And it's not my house. I just live here.'

He'd pulled into the drive and she clambered out of his car, wanting to distance herself from the man and his smart comments.

Not easy when he'd come to see his brother.

'He's probably sleeping,' she said. 'Would you like a cup of coffee?'

Grant came up behind her and touched her lightly on the shoulder.

'You're too good to be true, you know! You not only take in a stray you find in the bush, but now, when you should be dancing with joy at the prospect of getting rid of him, you're worried about disturbing his sleep.'

Sam shrugged.

It was better than admitting she wasn't exactly dancing with joy, for all she knew she should be.

'*Would* you like a cup of coffee? Some breakfast?'

He smiled at her, and his eyes twinkled again, exactly as Tom's did when he smiled.

'I'd like to see him first,' he said softly. 'If I promise not to wake him…'

She heard the anxiety in his voice and nodded, then led the way quietly down the wide hall which divided the up-stairs living and sleeping areas.

'He's in here,' she said, pushing open the guest-room door while her heart thudded erratically.

It's concern for him, she told herself, although she knew it was more complicated than that.

'Well, well,' Grant Hudson said softly, while a gruffness in his voice betrayed the depths of his emotion.

He crossed to the bed and stood looking down at his sleeping brother for a moment, then he walked quietly back towards Sam and followed her out the door.

'Damn fool!' he muttered. 'Damn stupid fool! When the hell will he learn to be content with life the way it is? Why does he have to go off on these mad adventures?'

Sam could think of a dozen reasons—maybe two dozen—to go off on mad adventures. Wasn't that what her solitary bush-walking was all about?

But she guessed that Grant Hudson didn't expect answers to his questions, so she put on the kettle and dug around in the freezer for some bun loaf. Coffee and fruity toast seemed like a good idea for breakfast.

'I thought I heard you come in. Mind you, the way this family leaves doors unlocked, anyone could walk in.'

Henry ambled into the kitchen, resplendent in red and blue striped pyjamas. He sounded calmer than when she'd last seen him, though when he caught sight of Grant, who'd wandered out onto the verandah to look down at the pool, all that changed.

'So, he's better now, is he?' he sneered. 'And found his clothes as well as his memory. That suit he's wearing isn't a hand-me-down of the boys.'

'That's—' Sam began, but Henry, spurred on by his simmering resentment of the intruder, had already launched himself towards the door.

'So, now you're better I presume you'll be taking yourself off,' he said to Grant. 'That's if you were ever sick!'

Sam watched Grant's facial expression switch from puzzled to wary.

'I'm Grant Hudson,' he said to Henry, and offered his hand.

'G-Grant?' Henry stuttered. 'If this is some devious idea you've hatched to get out of trouble with the police—'

Sam decided it was time to intervene. She reached out and grabbed Henry's arm, tugging him back into the kitchen.

'Surely you've had enough experience of twins to know they're different people,' she muttered at him. 'Look at his face. It's all one colour for a start.'

She didn't point out the other differences, like the fact that Tom had more laugh lines round his eyes and a little habit of smiling more with one side of his mouth than the other.

'This is the doctor from the hospital. I told you about him.'

Henry groaned and rested his head in his hands.

'This place is getting more like a madhouse every day,' he said, then he looked up at Sam. 'It won't do,' he told her. 'When we're married, you'll have to be like other people. Be normal!'

Sam wondered how she was supposed to reply to that little gem. Hitting him on the head with the breadboard was one solution.

Fortunately, before she could take action, a deep voice said, 'I don't think she does normal.'

She turned to find Tom standing there.

Smiling at her.

He must have made his way down the hall when she was separating the sparring men on the verandah.

She smiled back at him, because she couldn't help it, then saw his gaze shift from her towards the door.

'Grant! Hell, mate, but it's good to see you!'

The crackling noises in his voice made Sam's eyes water and she turned away, sniffing back the tears, while Grant crossed the kitchen in two strides and took his brother in his arms.

'Bloody idiot! Damn fool!'

The imprecations were so fondly spoken that Sam's eyes began to water once again.

'Well, at least you've found someone to take him off your hands,' Henry said.

'Why don't you go and get dressed?' Sam snapped at him, though it wasn't Henry's fault. All he'd done was point out the obvious.

An obvious that was making Sam feel very sad and lost.

CHAPTER TEN

THE two men moved to let Henry past, turning towards Sam, then, with Grant supporting his brother, they came into the kitchen.

Tom's face was alight with pleasure, and his eyes invited her to share his joy.

'I know him. I know Grant! I even remember why I'm here.'

He looked around, taking in the kitchen, and smiled at her.

'Well, not exactly here, although I can piece so much of it together. I can remember how I came to be up near the border. It was Kyogle, the little town on the southern side. We went to school there for a few years when Dad was at the hospital. After I checked in with the folks, I decided to drive north to see Grant. Catch up on what was happening for him in his new job. For some reason, going via Kyogle seemed like a good idea.'

'We used to walk in the mountains there. Go out along a forest road then bush-bash,' Grant reminded him.

Tom's smile made Sam feel even worse.

'I'm pretty sure that's what I intended doing. I remembered the road, and thought I'd go that way, detouring off the road from Kyogle to Brisbane. Have a walk. After all, you weren't expecting me, and I wasn't in any hurry.'

Unable to look at the pleasure in his face as he remembered things—or face the knowledge that the 'giving him back time' had arrived—Sam prised slices of frozen bun loaf apart and popped four into the heavy-duty toaster.

'Tea or coffee?' she asked, her voice falsely bright and cheery.

'Coffee,' they chorused.

She dug in the cupboard for the big coffeepot and, as she straightened, found Tom had come closer and was propped against the table.

'You don't have to feed us,' he said gently. 'You've done more than enough already.'

She shrugged her shoulders.

'I'm having coffee anyway,' she said, and ungracious didn't begin to describe her tone. 'Why don't you sit? Keep remembering. You were on the forest road.'

He frowned as if he'd picked up the edginess in her voice, but obeyed the order to sit, choosing a chair at the end of the table where he could look towards both her and Grant.

'I didn't get that far,' he said slowly, feeling out each word as if reading from a fuzzy script. 'There was an accident.'

'Accident?'

Again the word was chorused. Grant said it with surprise, but Henry, reappearing in a tidy suit and shiny shoes, spoke it with disbelief.

'A car had run off the road. The front end of it was rammed up against a tree.'

He frowned and squeezed his eyes shut for a moment, then opened them, and this time when he spoke Sam guessed he was describing an image that was becoming clearer in his mind.

'I couldn't see anyone. Thought they might be trapped inside. It looked as if it had just happened, although I don't know how I could have told something like that.'

'So you stopped,' Grant prompted.

His brother nodded.

'To offer help.' He frowned at his audience. 'That's all I can remember.'

He turned to Grant.

'Perhaps *I* had the car accident. That would explain the head injury. Could I be remembering it as someone else's accident.'

'Was this car accident before or after the bank robbery?' Henry asked, and Sam was surprised by the sarcasm in his voice.

Henry sarcastic?

But Grant diverted her from this puzzle. He was on his feet, moving around the table to stand behind his brother.

'I'm going to feel your head. Tell me where it hurts.'

Tom nodded, but was watching Sam.

'I'd forgotten about the bank robbery. The police coming. I'm so sorry for causing you so much trouble.'

Unable to stop herself, she smiled at him, but before she could assure him it had been her pleasure—well, in some ways it had been—he winced and grabbed his brother's hand.

'That hurts!' he said.

Then he grinned, producing a surprisingly cheerful expression for a man in pain.

'It wasn't an accident. Someone hit me. As I bent down to look into the car.'

Sam felt her heart falter at the thought of him in danger, but she held back the little gasp of protest, not wanting to interrupt his recollections.

'I straightened up, lashed out, but then another person was there.'

'There are two lumps on your thick skull,' Grant told him. 'You were hit again.'

'But had there been an accident or was it staged?' Sam

asked. Better to be thinking about his story than the danger he'd been in.

'I'd say it was staged,' Tom said, the words measured again as if he was reviewing the tape of his memories. 'Perhaps their car had broken down, because it's hardly the place you'd choose to steal a vehicle for a bank robbery. By pushing their car into the tree and staying out of sight, they'd ensure someone would stop to investigate.'

He paused again, then nodded as if satisfied by his thoughts.

'If a car with more than one person had stopped, they could have remained hidden. Waiting until an unsuspecting single driver came along.'

'But how did he get from there to the national park—and across the border?'

Grant nodded and smiled at Sam's question as if he'd been about to ask it himself. Once again she noted the strange phenomenon that his smile did nothing to her nerves. She buttered some toast and waited for Tom to answer.

'I imagine they baulked at leaving my unconscious body by the side of the road. It's well used and if I was found an alert would go out for the car. They must have detoured onto the forest road I'd intended taking, and gone as far as they could to reduce the chance of my being found, then dumped me. I think I can vaguely recall some argument to the effect that they should draw the line at murder.'

Sam shuddered but Tom seemed more relieved, remembering, than upset by what had happened.

'After which,' Tom added, 'I must have blundered through the bush, eventually falling down the cliff in front of Sam, and the rest we know.'

He seemed so pleased to have put the pieces together

that Sam was tempted to smile again, but Grant was looking serious.

'Where had you been before that?' he asked his brother.

'On the Mentawai Islands, of course. Have you forgotten I was going there to work with the hylobates, the primate they call the bilou?'

Tom smiled at Sam as she put a plate of toast on the table. 'Female bilous have the most beautiful song. On a clear morning, you hear it echoing through the forest as the mother and her children hurl themselves through the branches of the tall trees.'

And Sam, although she knew she had to give him back, returned the smile, for the thought of listening to a monkey singing in the forest made perfect sense to her.

It was the oneness thing again.

'The kettle's boiling, Sam,' Henry prompted, and she pulled herself together.

Tom's married, she reminded herself, turning away to pour boiling water into the coffeepot and find mugs and milk and sugar.

She set the lot, with small plates, knives, honey and jam, on the table, then leant back against the sink.

Grant was asking technical questions and, as far as Sam could tell, getting acceptable answers.

'And Jocelyn,' she said to Tom, when she couldn't stand the strain of not knowing any longer. 'Can you remember her?'

The blue of his eyes was immediately shielded by lowered lashes.

'Jocelyn!' he muttered, then he opened his eyes to look at Sam again.

'You must admit I didn't ever forget her,' he said. 'I told you about Jocelyn, didn't I?'

'Frequently!'

But if he noticed the dryness in her voice he didn't react, turning instead to his brother.

'How did I leave things with her? *Were* we engaged? I seem to remember there being talk of it, perhaps when I came home. Yet somehow I connect her up with wanting to walk in the forest.'

Grant grinned at him.

'You always said you made decisions better in the forest than anywhere else. Myself, I go for beaches. Long stretches of white sand, completely deserted—that's where a man can find most answers to his life.'

Sam listened but felt a shiver work its way up her spine. She was definitely a forest decision-maker herself.

It's coincidence, like finding Grant working at my hospital. Just because we choose the same type of isolation for decision-making doesn't make us soul mates!

'So it was Jocelyn and that final dread commitment I was going to think about,' Tom said, quite happily for a man who was wearing a wedding ring. 'Well, I certainly sorted that out!'

He took a slice of toast then passed the plate to Henry.

'In what way?' Henry asked, his voice tight, as if he'd been drawn into the conversation against his will.

'I don't think she's the woman for me,' Tom announced. Then he turned to Grant. 'Is she going to be very upset? I've an idea—more a feeling—that she gave up on me when I announced I was doing this last trip. Was she furious? Did she take it out on you?'

Grant shook his head.

'I think she was more disturbed when you arrived home then climbed into your car and headed for Brisbane without so much as contacting her to say hello.'

'How did she know I was home?'

'You were due home, Tom. You had a plane ticket. Mum

met you at the airport, told you Jocelyn was expecting to
see you, and you announced you had to see me first. That's
the last any of us heard of you until your photo turned up
on the most-wanted list.'

'It seems a very callous way to treat a woman, even if
she wasn't your fiancée,' Henry said, disapproval dripping
from his voice. 'And what about that wedding ring? Was
it how to tell this poor Jocelyn woman you'd married someone else that you had to think about?'

But Tom didn't reply. He was staring at the ring.

'Damn! Another hole in the Swiss cheese.'

Grant chuckled.

'I wouldn't worry about it at the moment. According to
your rescuer, I was in a Swiss-cheese hole as well, and you
remember me now.'

'Once seen, never forgotten,' Tom joked, slapping his
brother on the back.

As Sam saw the camaraderie in the gesture, and heard
the love in his voice, she felt a sense of desolation sweep
over her, a regret so strong it made her bones feel heavy
and her body ache.

She made more toast, kept making it, for Sean appeared,
closely followed by Pete. Their delight at finding another
set of twins soon developed into serious mayhem as they
propounded all the fun they could have pulling 'double
twin' stunts.

'The permutations and combinations are awesome,' Sean
declared. 'I don't suppose one of you would like to marry
Sam and have more twins, then we could do a combined
family thing with no one ever knowing who was who.'

'Don't be ridiculous,' Sam told him, at the same time as
Henry declared, 'But Sam's marrying me.'

And although this wasn't the right time or place, Sam

knew she couldn't let Henry go on thinking it would happen.

'No, Henry, I'm not,' she said gently. 'I'm sorry and I'll try to explain later.'

But her words, and certainly the gentleness, were all but drowned out by Tom, who also replied to Henry.

'No, she's not,' he said firmly. 'She's marrying me.'

'You're already married,' Sam reminded him, then realised it had been the wrong thing to say.

'I don't feel married,' he replied, turning to Grant for clarification.

'Don't look at me! There are some holes I can't fill in for you,' his brother said. 'You've been on leave, been over in the islands for six months, and wedding rings usually have some significance.'

'You can always get divorced,' Pete comforted him. 'That's if you ever work out who you married. Then you can marry Sam and have twins and we can—'

'Stop it this instant!' Sam said. 'You two always have to go too far.' She glared at Tom. 'And you and Grant are probably just as bad. Thinking this twin thing is some kind of gigantic lark—a joke you play on the rest of the world.'

And with that she stormed out, before she *did* hit someone with the breadboard—or burst into tears, which would probably be worse.

So she fled, heading for her bedroom, then remembered it wasn't hers right now, and sought refuge in Gran's room instead.

A gentle tap on the door half an hour later was followed by Tom's voice asking if he could come in.

'No!' she said, using every ounce of inner strength to form the simple syllable. 'If you want to say goodbye, say it through the door. I'll go first. Goodbye.'

She heard his soft chuckle.

'Did I hear you add "and good riddance" under your breath, sweet Sam?'

She pushed her face into a pillow so she wouldn't answer, knowing that once a dialogue was begun she'd weaken and walk out to see him one more time.

Then the 'goodbye' she prayed for, yet didn't want to hear, came softly through the old wooden panels.

'And thank you,' he added.

She strained her ears to pick up the tap and shuffle of his movement down the hall, out across the verandah. And even when she couldn't hear it, she imagined it, all the way down the front steps and across to Grant's car.

The after-effects of the bus accident kept her so busy at work she had little time to brood, and being busy meant exhaustion followed, so she slept soundly each day. Fortunately Gran had returned from her cruise and was in command at home, so Sam could sleep and eat and concentrate on not thinking—moving like an automaton through each day.

Henry, when she'd finally sat down with him and apologised for letting things drag on so long, had seemed more relieved than distressed by her decision. In fact, if the number of times he mentioned the new bookkeeper he had in his office were any guide, he was a fair way to falling in love himself.

Himself?

She wasn't in love!

Love was something that grew between two people. Based on friendship, and trust, and mutual interests, and understanding. You had to really know someone to fall in love.

She saw Grant occasionally, when one of the regular crises in a neuro patient brought him on a night visit to the

ICU. Craig Greenway, the patient who'd had the spinal epidural clot removed, had been moved upstairs to a general surgical ward, but William and another of Grant's patients, who'd had an aneurysm clipped, both still needed more intensive care.

'Tom's coming back from Sydney on Friday,' Grant said to Sam, four weeks after Tom had shuffled out of her life. Although she'd been careful not to appear too interested when he'd spoken of Tom from time to time, her anxiety betrayed her this time.

She grasped his arm as she asked, 'What about his job? Do the specialists think he's not well enough to go back to work? What have they found?'

Grant grinned at her and patted the hand she'd forgotten to remove from his white coat.

'He's fine. I told you he'd had that second bout of fever with the dengue but apparently it's completely left his system now and my mother tells me he's starting to put on weight. He's also been passed fit to return to work mid-March, which was when he was due to start back. But I know he'd like to see you.' He paused. 'To thank you properly. After all, I did whisk him away a bit suddenly. And when he phones he can't seem to catch you at home.'

Not with Gran and the twins instructed to say she was unavailable to anyone who phoned!

'He doesn't have to thank me properly,' Sam replied. 'I only did what anyone else would have done.'

'Of course,' Grant said, but she knew that if she looked, his eyes would be twinkling, and although they were different eyes, the twinkling upset her.

She refused to look.

'I'm on duty this weekend,' she said to him, crossing her fingers behind her back. 'Maybe some other time.'

She hurried away, making a mental note to see Wendy

and work out who she could change shifts with so it wouldn't be a real lie. Most people hated weekend shifts so swapping shouldn't be difficult.

'You can't hide from the man for the rest of your life,' Wendy told her, when she made her request.

Her friendship with the new neurosurgeon had been so obvious she'd been forced to explain some of the story to her workmates.

'I can try, and I can start with this weekend,' Sam responded. 'Now, who's most likely to agree to swap?'

'Jenny Simpson's going to a wedding on Friday at five and was going to come on to work after it. She'll be happy to give you Friday night. Saturday night's harder because casuals work Saturdays and they like the extra pay.'

'Friday will do for a start,' Sam said. 'Will you see Jenny or will I?'

They sorted it out and Sam told herself she was relieved.

For a Friday, it was relatively quiet—no new patients admitted, no crises with the ones they had—so when, through the glass windows of the room where she was tending her patient, she saw Grant turn up, she was surprised.

A quick glance at the clock told her it was almost the end of her shift. If he'd come to try to persuade her to see Tom...

She turned away, but watched surreptitiously as he chatted to the nurse at the monitors, then he looked up and she had to look quickly away before he caught her studying him.

Using him to bring back another face.

'I'm on and you're off,' a nurse Sam hadn't met—perhaps a casual who worked weekends—came bouncing through the door. 'What do I need to know?'

Sam outlined what she'd already written on the patient's chart. As well as the big things the monitors checked, the

little details of nursing—the suctioning, cleaning the patient's mouth, seeing to the care of his or her body—were
all vitally important in an ICU.

Eventually she left the room, and all but ran into Grant.

Only it wasn't Grant, it was Tom.

Wasn't it?

She looked at him—suit pants, white coat, stethoscope
poking out of his pocket.

He was dressed like Grant but it wasn't. It was most
definitely Tom.

'What are you doing here?' she hissed at him, some protective instinct working to hide the switch from the nursing
staff.

She didn't wait for him to answer, but hurried him towards the tearoom.

'Of all the cheek. Impersonating a medical officer!'

'I am a medical officer,' he reminded her. 'Any number
of degrees and citations to prove it.'

'You're pretending to be Grant!' she reminded him,
reaching the tearoom and finding it full of nurses coming
either on or off duty.

'We can't talk here!' she fumed, and pushed him back
to the door, steering him out of the ward, towards the lifts.

'Now can we talk?' he asked, when they pushed into a
lift also crowded with change of shift staff.

'No!' Sam whispered at him, although right now her anger was losing the battle with the other stuff happening in
her body. The physical heat and ripples and generally fla-
grant delight in being with him again.

'I've never kissed you, do you realise that?' He murmured the question in a seductive undertone that made her
shiver and flush with heat at the same time.

'Yes, and you probably never will,' she muttered back
at him.

'The lift's so crowded no one would notice,' he persisted.

'They would when you yelled,' she told him.

The eyes that had begun all the trouble did their puzzled look.

'Why would I yell?'

'Because I'd kick you.'

He drew back but smiled down at her and she realised his lips were just as devastating as his eyes. In fact, for a fraction of a second she regretted her stand on the kick.

Remembered that imagined kiss when his lips had taken possession of hers...

'You've a streak of sadism in you, sweet Sam,' he complained. 'That's not the first violence you've threatened to direct at my person. Pushing me down cliffs, hitting me on the head, kicking my injured ankle.'

His voice grew louder as he listed his complaints and Sam was glad enough people had got off to reduce his audience to one bored-looking porter, an orderly and a couple of giggling nurses.

Not wanting to draw further attention to herself and her companion, she held her tongue, satisfying herself with directing a fulminating glare at him.

His answering look of mock contrition didn't fool her—not for one minute.

'I've got a hire car,' he said, when they eventually emerged into the basement car park. 'Seemed easier than trying to juggle the use of Grant's around his work times and emergencies. I did warn him about neurosurgery. Suggested dermatology. You never get called out at night to look at someone's rash. I'll drive you home.'

Sam considered arguing then realised she was shaking so much she'd be a danger on the road and gave in, although, once again, they were barely on their way before she remembered she'd whisked him out so fast she'd forgotten her handbag.

'Is it in a locker?' Tom asked, when she demanded they return.

'Of course it is,' she muttered, *déjà vu* continuing.

'Then that's OK,' he told her, unconsciously echoing his brother's lack of concern.

Traffic lights halted their progress and he turned to look at her.

Again the memory of that imagined kiss returned, and she leaned towards him, willing it to happen, although she knew she shouldn't.

'How did you know it was me?' he asked, jerking her back to reality with his question. 'My face is tanned all one colour. The stitches are out and the scar's more under my chin than on it. For which I thank you, ma'am.' He smiled and then, when she didn't respond, the smile turned to a frown.

'Do you see Grant so often you could pick up the difference?'

He sounded slightly put out, but Sam wasn't going to ease his peevishness by telling him about the ripples.

Not yet.

'I suppose, having grown up with the twins, I see the little things.'

'Like what?' They were on their way again.

'Your face is slightly leaner—that could be the result of your time away, but I feel it's natural.'

'That's all? I've got a thinner face? You take one look and say to yourself, "no, it's the thin-faced one. Not Grant."' He shook his head. 'I don't believe you.'

'Then you can stay disbelieving as far as I'm concerned,' Sam told him.

She folded her arms and turned her head, pretending to be absorbed in the houses and shops she passed every day.

But Tom didn't pass them every day.

'How do you know the way?' she asked.

He slipped her a smile that made her sorry she wasn't still watching houses. It weakened her resolve to remain aloof from him.

'I went to visit you last night,' he replied, reaching out and letting one finger graze her bare arm. 'I met your gran, and saw the twins, but you were at work.'

She rubbed the place where his finger had been, trying to remove the tingling in her skin. There was far too much to be resolved to give in to tingling skin, no matter how her body was responding to his presence.

'I told Grant I'd be at work.'

'Yes!'

'What do you mean, yes?' Sam demanded.

Another smile was eased her way.

'Avoidance tactics, Sam? Swapping shifts to make your story true? I've been around hospitals a long time, I know how it's done.'

'I can't believe Grant asked if I swapped shifts. The cheek of the man.'

Tom pulled into the drive and stopped at the bottom of the steps.

'He didn't check to see if you'd swapped, but he'd found out earlier that you'd be off duty this weekend. I asked him to check on your roster. It was a matter of timing my visit.'

Could he really have wanted to see her so badly?

To say thank you, or something more?

Dared she hope...?

She looked at him, studying the face she'd seen revealed, bit by bit, during his brief incursion into her life.

It was very like the one she saw in dreams, although in

the dreams it was always slightly magnified—caught in the split second before he kissed her.

'I didn't want to see you,' she admitted quietly.

He didn't move yet somehow she felt comfort, as if some essence of his being was reaching out to hold her. To comfort and protect her.

'I know you didn't,' he said gently. 'But it seemed to me there was too much left unsaid. Too much I'd had no right to say before this.'

He held his left hand towards her and she saw the white band of skin where the wedding ring had been.

Her heart faltered, torn between hope and disbelief.

'Quickie divorce?' She spoke lightly, hoping to break the tension straining in the air between them.

'Annulment,' he replied, his lips tilting into the little half-smile that made her knees go trembly. He rested his hand on the steering-wheel, and she saw his fingers tighten on the plastic.

She realised he was as tense as she was. Holding on to his cool with difficulty.

'Remember the pigs?'

'Pigs and marriage?'

His fingers relaxed and the smile became full-blown.

'Exactly. Only the explanation was simple. I'd been over in the islands for extended periods of time before, and the villagers with whom I stayed seemed to feel a single man was an insult to their women. I was offered sisters, daughters, cousins and widows. All with their dowries of either pigs or fish-traps! The ring was protection from the offers. And from giving offence by saying no. I bought it in Singapore on my way through. Scout's honour.'

Sam chuckled at his accompanying salute, though the strong flutter of relief she felt inside her was no laughing

matter. And the joy she was feeling shouldn't be so un-
bounded, should it?

Wasn't there something else? Some other consideration
to be taken into account before she gave in to the simmering excitement building in her blood and thudding in her
chest?

She looked into his eyes and what she saw there only
deepened her delight. Tempted her to give in to the wishes
of her heart and the increasingly urgent demands of her
body, and kiss the man.

But…

She forced herself to think through the haze of attraction,
to find the other obstacle they had to clear.

Jocelyn!

'What about Jocelyn?' The words came out so quietly
she wondered if he'd hear them. Then she saw his smile
fade, and his eyes grow watchful.

He reached out, as if to take Sam's hand, then sat back
again, studying her face as he explained.

'Jocelyn has been around in my life—in our lives, in fact,
she's Grant's friend as well as mine—for a long time. Grant
took her out for a while, then he got stuck into speciality
studies and I was available—'

'So you swapped?' Sam's outrage made the words sharp-
edged.

'Jocelyn swapped,' Tom said firmly. 'She shifted alle-
giance to me and, although she stayed close to Grant, when
I was in town, and when I had time, we saw each other.'

'When you had time you saw each other?' Sam's empathy was now with Jocelyn. 'What a way to treat a
woman! Like a convenience.'

Tom looked shocked.

'It wasn't like that at all. She saw other men. Neither of
us were committed—well, not totally.'

'Yet she came up here, looking for you.'

Tom looked puzzled, the crease she'd first noticed at the bottom of the cliff reappearing between his eyebrows.

She resisted the urge to smooth it away as he repeated her words.

'Came up here?'

'I assume she lives in Sydney,' Sam muttered, increasingly irritated by the conversation she'd initiated. 'Doubt you'd have been flying to Brisbane whenever you were free to take advantage of her availability.'

The crease disappeared and he smiled again.

'She did live in Sydney, but while I was away she decided she needed a new life, so she applied for a job in Brisbane. She was due to start and was only waiting until I got home so she could tell me about it. That's why she was so annoyed when I disappeared without seeing her.'

His smile broadened to beaming proportions, as if this final explanation had brought his life to the point where everything was rosy.

And while a lot of what he'd said had brought a similar sense of rosiness to Sam, there was plenty more ground to be covered before she could be sure that what she felt was not one-sided.

Her heart was hesitant to ask, afraid to know, but the kiss she wanted so badly, the embrace she knew she'd never want to end, would have to wait.

'So?' she prompted, hoping to hear words she'd only imagined hearing from a man. Words of love and passion and desire.

The beaming smile faded, and a hint of the crease returned between his eyebrows.

'So, what?'

He sounded so genuinely perplexed, she had to hide a smile.

'So why are you telling me this?' she teased.

The crease became a real frown.

'So you know I'm free,' he told her, exasperation breaking through. 'So you understand it's OK.'

'What's OK?' she persisted, though hiding her smile was becoming more difficult, especially when her heart was skipping beats and breathing had become a challenge.

'You and I. It's OK to—' He stopped abruptly, desperation dimming the light in his eyes. Then he rallied, seized her by the shoulders and growled, '*This* is OK!' And bent to kiss her on the lips.

Hard.

Sam pretended it was just a kiss but it took all her strength not to whimper a protest when he drew back and looked sternly into her eyes.

'I've been wanting to do that since I opened my eyes at the bottom of the cliff and found you looking down at me. And don't pretend you haven't felt it, because a one-sided attraction couldn't possibly be this compelling. You *must* be feeling what I'm feeling. For a start, tell me how you knew I wasn't Grant. The truth, now.'

She let a little bit of the smile escape and snuggled closer to him.

'You've become very authoritarian all of a sudden. Is this the real you?'

The glimmer of light in his eyes teased her heart, and the corner of his lips twitched when he repeated, more as a request, an appeal, than a demand, 'Tell me?'

Sam felt confusion heat her body and climb to paint her cheeks, but as she had needed words to reassure her, so now did he.

'It's different—being near Grant.'

She looked hopefully into Tom's eyes, unwilling, perhaps unable, to put the feeling into words. Would he understand? Accept such a limp statement as enough?

But life, and particularly the love aspect of it, wasn't meant to be easy.

'How?' he asked.

Sam studied the eyes that had first snagged her attention, and what she saw there made her tremble. She snuggled even closer and leaned up to kiss him, but again it was he who stopped first.

'Different in what way?' he whispered to her, and Sam, her nerves strung so tight she expected to hear them snapping any minute, gave up the search for fancy explanations.

And the protective instincts that had suggested she might be making a fool of herself.

'He doesn't make me hum! Not smell hum, or make a noise hum, but an inside kind of humming. When I'm near Grant, it's like being near anyone. Nothing happens inside my skin. No ripples, no tingles, no vibrations.'

She spoke defiantly. After all, it was the truth. Tom Hudson could make what he wanted of it.

She glanced at his face and saw sheer joy light his eyes.

'I knew it couldn't be one-sided,' he said, and she had time to note the satisfaction in his voice before he once again claimed her lips. Only this time the kiss was soft, lingering, exploratory, and so seductive that Sam gave herself up to the glory of it, kissing him back with a fervour she hadn't known existed in her normally quiescent body.

CHAPTER ELEVEN

'IT MIGHTN'T mean anything, you know,' Sam whispered, as she drew back from the kiss what seemed like a month later but apparently was still the same morning.

'In what way, mightn't mean anything?' Tom demanded.

'Well, we were thrown together. Had to depend on each other. The two of us against the odds. It was an adversity friendship.'

'It didn't stop there, though, did it?' he reminded her, and she let him kiss her to prove the point.

Kissed him back because it was easier than thinking, although, eventually, thoughts broke through again.

'What you're feeling might be gratitude,' she suggested, afraid something so rapturously delightful couldn't possibly be reciprocated.

'What I'm feeling is an attraction so strong it's killing me, woman!' he retorted, growling to give the words added emphasis.

'It could be lust,' she countered, still unconvinced, although another kiss, definitely reciprocated, suggested it was more.

'Rubbish!' said the man who'd tumbled into her life. 'You've poured enough cold water over my pretensions for lust to have vanished under the weight of your denial. Threatening me with violence, not saying goodbye, refusing to take my calls. A lesser man might have broken under the strain.'

He used his smile to full effect.

'Surely persistence deserves some reward.'

Knowing, from the first few, the effect his kisses had on her brain, she should have avoided the next one. But her lips seemed to want it, her heart ached for it, and her body fitted itself comfortably against his in spite of the limitations of space in the front seat of the rental car.

'Like this?' she whispered, and this time she kissed him.

'Or this?' she murmured later, running the tip of her tongue across his jawline before nibbling at his ear lobe.

His answer was a strangled groan, uttered a split second before he reclaimed her lips.

'They're getting better at it,' a too-familiar voice remarked, and Sam, shocked by her own abandoned behaviour, dragged herself back into her seat. A glance out the window revealed an audience of two—the twins were sitting on the front steps.

'A full seven minutes. You'd wonder they could breathe.'

Sean was holding his watch in his hand, stopwatch fashion, and was responsible for this unwanted opinion.

'See what you've done,' Sam said crossly to Tom.

He chuckled at her discomfort, then opened the car door and clambered out.

'Why don't you two do something useful, like making breakfast? Something hearty would be nice. Pancakes, bacon, eggs, perhaps a sausage.'

'If a couple of kisses gives him that much of an appetite, heaven knows what a good night in bed will do,' Pete remarked, then, as Sam erupted from the car, intent on bodily harm, they raced away.

'It's their way of showing they're happy for us,' Tom said, sliding his arm around Sam's shoulders and tucking her body in close to his.

'Is there an us?' Sam asked him, looking into the blue eyes that had haunted her dreams for too long.

'How could there not be?' he asked. 'It's like the old songs. Two hearts that beat as one.'

'You live in Sydney,' she reminded him, as much to bring her feet back down onto solid ground as to raise more objections. 'It's geographically impossible.'

They were halfway up the steps when she spoke—and finally snapped Tom's patience.

He swung her into his arms and carried her up the remaining steps, then sat down on one of the verandah chairs and held her on his knee.

'Now, are you going to stop thinking up objections and get with the programme here, or am I going to have to put you over my knee and spank you into submission?'

Up close, Sam could see a tiny scar running up through one eyebrow and her fingers, beyond control of her brain, crept up to touch it. Then down to investigate the scar beneath his chin.

Which should have been enough, but the shapely lips, delineated by a whitish line, drew them on, and with a fingertip she traced the edges.

'We barely know each other,' she whispered, wondering now if any one person deserved as much happiness as she'd begun to feel.

'We'll remedy that,' he promised.

'We'll be multiplying our chances of having twins,' she reminded him, almost smiling because somehow her mind was beginning to accept what her body already knew.

'We could take out insurance,' he said gravely, then he smiled and said, 'I love you, Sam.'

'Breakfast in ten minutes if you want to have a shower.' Sean made the announcement from the front door. He paused, perhaps wondering if they were going to provide more entertainment for him, but when they both glared at him he shrugged and turned away, swinging back to say to

Sam, 'And I'd change into something else if I were you. When the twins ask what you were wearing when their father proposed, you don't want to have to tell them it was a Betadine-stained uniform.'

Sam reached for a shell that decorated the little table beside the chair, but before she could throw it her brother had disappeared.

'With any luck they'll be girl twins,' Tom said, and she sighed.

'You're just as bad as he is,' she told the man she loved.

Then she leaned forward and pressed her lips to his, felt her body melt and mould itself to his shape—felt doubt vanish and a deep, enduring certainty creep in.

They'd need time to get to know each other properly but, after all, they had a lifetime.

MILLS & BOON®

Makes any time special™

Mills & Boon publish 29 new titles every month. Select from...

Modern Romance™   Tender Romance™

Sensual Romance™

Medical Romance™   Historical Romance™

MAT2

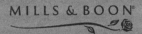

MILLS & BOON®

Medical Romance™

CLAIMED: ONE WIFE *by Meredith Webber*

Book two of The Australian Doctors duo

Neurosurgeon Grant Hudson knows that fraternisation between colleagues can break hearts, ruin careers and even lives. Yet for Dr Sally Cochrane, he is prepared to break his own rule. Sally, however, has her own reasons for keeping him out of her life...

A NURSE'S FORGIVENESS *by Jessica Matthews*

Book one of Nurses Who Dare trilogy

Marta Wyman is not going to let Dr Evan Gallagher pressurise her into meeting up with her grandfather. No matter how handsome, polite and charming Evan is he will have a long wait before she changes her mind— or gives in to her desires...

THE ITALIAN DOCTOR *by Jennifer Taylor*

Dalverston General Hospital

Resentment simmered between Luke Fabrizzi and Maggie Carr when her family tried to introduce them with marriage in mind. But a staged relationship in order to avert their families led to a truce—and another battle against their true feelings!

On sale 4th May 2001

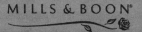

Medical Romance™

NURSE IN NEED *by Alison Roberts*

Emergency nurse Amy Brooks rushed into an engagement when she realised she wanted a family of her own—then she met Dr Tom Barlow. She had to end the engagement and Tom was delighted—but was his love for Amy the real reason?

THE GENTLE TOUCH *by Margaret O'Neill*

Jeremy is asked to persuade Veronica Lord into letting him treat her. Just as he gains her trust, Jeremy discovers that he was present when she had her accident and could have helped her. Will she ever be able to forgive him, let alone love him?

SAVING SUZANNAH *by Abigail Gordon*

Until Dr Lafe Hilliard found her, Suzannah Scott believed she had nothing left. Lafe helped her to rebuild her life and all he wanted in return was honesty. But if Suzannah revealed her past, she risked not only losing his professional respect, but his love...

On sale 4th May 2001

4 FREE
books and a surprise gift!

We would like to take this opportunity to thank you for reading this Mills & Boon® book by offering you the chance to take FOUR more specially selected titles from the Medical Romance™ series absolutely FREE! We're also making this offer to introduce you to the benefits of the Reader Service™—

- ★ FREE home delivery
- ★ FREE gifts and competitions
- ★ FREE monthly Newsletter
- ★ Exclusive Reader Service discounts
- ★ Books available before they're in the shops

Accepting these FREE books and gift places you under no obligation to buy, you may cancel at any time, even after receiving your free shipment. Simply complete your details below and return the entire page to the address below. *You don't even need a stamp!*

YES! Please send me 4 free Medical Romance books and a surprise gift. I understand that unless you hear from me, I will receive 6 superb new titles every month for just £2.49 each, postage and packing free. I am under no obligation to purchase any books and may cancel my subscription at any time. The free books and gift will be mine to keep in any case.

M1ZEA

Ms/Mrs/Miss/Mr ....Initials.................................
                                                                 BLOCK CAPITALS PLEASE

Surname ....

Address ....

....

....Postcode.....................

Send this whole page to:
UK: FREEPOST CN81, Croydon, CR9 3WZ
EIRE: PO Box 4546, Kilcock, County Kildare (stamp required)